MERRY & BRIGHT
A Callisto Christmas

<////JJ_HYND>

For all the girls who grew up watching cliché Hallmark Christmas movies this is for you. Except spicier. And with alien dick.

<///JJ_HYND>

AUTHOR'S NOTE

I am British, and thus this book is written in
British English.

Which is similar, and yet different, from US English. These are not
spelling mistakes, simply a difference between the two written
languages.

<///JJ_HYND>

<////JJ_HYND>

CHAPTER ONE
8 Sleeps til Christmas

"Darling!" Mum starts, "Oh, the Christmas Light Switch-on! You should have seen it, Dear. Aunt Marge practically fainted," Mum chortles to herself, talking over Dad.

"Hi, Mum," I say, "Poor Aunt Marge."

My workstation beeps, pulling my attention to the next round of chemical analysis charts popping up on screen.

"And your father—"

"*Your* Mother stood watching in hysterics. Meanwhile, I'm exposing myself to half the population of Southend Pier." I can practically hear the displeased eyebrow raise accompanying his haughty huff.

I slump back into my office chair. "Poor Southend," I say as I double tap the chemical analysis charts.

"Hardly *half* the population. A handful at best, Darling," Mum laughs again, "Completely unaware he was."

More lab results pop up on screen. Most likely taken from today's backlog of crime scene evidence left over from the night shift.

"A lucky few got an eyeful." You can hear the smug smirk in Dad's voice.

"The lucky ones were too busy with the fireworks," Mum scoffs, "Margie definitely had the shock of her life."

<//MERRY&BRIGHT>

A small smile tugs at my lips as I listen to their antics. "How is old Aunt Marge, again?" I ask.

"Still old as dirt," Dad chortles.

I hear a loud swatting sound, swiftly followed by Dad's grunt of pain.

"Don't be uncouth, Rupert."

A laugh escapes me. I do miss their antics.

"Aunt Marge is so sad she'll miss you at Christmas, but we're looking forward to seeing you, Dear," my mother's voice rings in my ears as I swipe through to the next chemical analysis chart.

"Christmas...?" I echo back to my parents, only half listening as I start typing a data summary for a cherry blossom found at a crime scene in Callisto suburbia.

Prunus Serrulata... I type.

"Of course!" scoffs Dad, "Did you think we'd *miss* Christmas with our darling girl?"

I keep typing.

Native to Japan, United Nations Earth.

"Christmas is two weeks away. It's too late to request leave from the lab," I say as my fingers glide across the keyboard.

Cell abnormalities consistent with growth in lower gravity environments such as Callisto or Ganymede.

I pause, my hands hovering over the keyboard.

"Besides, the transports will all be fully booked by now."

"Of course, Darling."

Another data analysis comes through. Kinetic bullet striation comparison. I sigh. *I'm not convinced there is a night shift at this point.* You'd think a colony of a little under one hundred thousand would generate less paperwork.

<////JJ_HYND>

"It's not like the police shut down over the holidays," I argue.

"We understand how important your work is to you," Mum coos.

"Thanks, Mum." I fiddle with the hem of my cardigan, rolling the knitted fabric between my finger and thumb. "Which is why I won't make it back this year."

"Exactly!" she exclaims excitedly.

"Exactly...?" I echo back confused.

"Which is why we are—"

"Coming to you instead," Mum finishes for Dad in her trademark sing-song voice.

"Oh..." I send the compiled report over to Inspector Peters. W*ait, what?*

My fingers halt over my workstation. Tongue paralyses in my mouth. Throat drier than the Sahara (pre-reforestation efforts) in an instant. My mind blue screens, freezing.

"What?" I mumble, barely coherently.

They ignore the question.

"We got our hands on some tickets. *SolGlider,* First Class."

"Spared no expense," Dad chirps in, "It's not every day you visit your daughter on another planet!"

"Moon," I correct absently.

"Aliens and humans living together! Eating together. Frolicking about," Mum exclaims, "Who would have thought!" She chuckles to herself.

"We aren't frolicking..." I drift off into my thoughts.

My parents will be *here*. *On Callisto*. In my tiny domicile. They will want to see where I work, where I live, my friends, my...

<///MERRY&BRIGHT>

"I can't wait to meet your new man friend," Mum sings out to me in that high pitch tone she does when she's excited.

Oh fuck.

"I think they call it boyfriend, Darling," corrects Dad.

"He's not a boy though," Mum stammers.

"It's an expression, Dear," Dad interrupts.

"He's a man. Right? Alison?" Mum's interrogation begins.

Fuck.

"How old is he, Darling?"

Fuckity. Fuck. Fuck.

"Do aliens say boyfriend?" Excitement rings in her tone.

"Mate?" I offer, my brain functioning on autopilot alone.

"How primal."

"He's an alien?" gasps Dad, scandalised.

"She's not on Earth, Rupert. He must be." She's practically giddy.

"We try not to call them aliens," I amend. My politically correct office training coming to the forefront of my mind.

"At least not to their face, eh?" Dad chortles. "Oof," He grunts out from another swatting.

The ambient lighting of my office pulses, alerting me to someone at the door, awaiting my response.

"Mum, Dad, I've got to go. I'm at work."

"Okay, Darling. Speak soon."

The call disconnects in a frenzy of 'mwah-mwah's. The lit-up display of my Glass blinks out of existence and I'm left alone staring into the void.

<////JJ_HYND>

Slowly, my eyes adjust until my workstation comes back into focus. I become painfully aware of the leaning tower of sealed evidence boxes pushed up against the wall, of the five cold coffee cups with varying levels of fluid contents, and at least a week's worth of noodle boxes stacked up in the corner.

"Computer, open door," I call out as I shut down my workstation and shove the noodle boxes into the bin. A half-hearted attempt at portraying a semblance of work/life balance.

"*A'lors Tuk, L-E.*" Inspector Quercus saunters in. His typical gaudy Hawaiian shirt has been swapped for a Christmas themed one of palm trees wrapped in twinkling lights and candy canes. The festive red clashes with his emerald-green skin.

It takes a moment for my *RenChip* to wake up; the first translation coming in slow, "Warm greetings, L-E."

The non-humans seem to struggle with my name as it tends to translate into monosyllabic sounds through their implanted translators. Universal translation is not a precise science.

"Good morning, Inspector," I say.

Many a night has been spent pondering the racrurian people since I arrived on Callisto.

How are they so tall when their home world is approximate to Earth in its G-rating? Why the evolutionary need for green skin? Is their epidermis rich in chlorophyll like, the once wild and prolific flora of Earth was? Why the tail?

Quercus flops down in the office chair adjacent; his festive button-up drooping open to reveal the pistol holstered at his hip.

<//MERRY&BRIGHT>

My eyes are drawn to the weapon; at his laissez-faire attitude towards it. I may work for the police, but I rarely leave the lab. I've never carried a gun, let alone fired one off at another living being. The closest I've come is watching my lab tech fire a ballistics test through jelly.

Quercus' tail glides leisurely side to side. Relaxed and unbothered.

He frowns at my silence and likely vacant expression.

"Paradise is frowning?" Quercus asks, my *RenChip* implant now whirred up and translating only a few moments behind.

"Trouble in paradise?" I offer.

"Ah, yes," Quercus replies in jilted English. The 's' sound struggling to escape around his enlarged canines.

His short black hair frames his strong, angular face. A deep, piney green with emerald cheeks and a purple cosmos in his eyes. He offers me a toothy grin.

"My parents are visiting," I tell him as my mind continues reeling.

"For Winter tree?" My translator picks up the very literal meanings of his words.

I nod.

"Festivities." He smiles. "Jewels tells me it is a party to exchange gifts and clothe a tree." He frowns. "Do you require some flora?"

"Not exactly," I sigh exasperated, "I require a boyfriend."

Quercus toothy grin transforms into a beaming smile. "I get you a Huckleberry."

A Huckleberry? What is this? The Wild West? Jeez... Someone really needs to start monitoring Quercus' access to old Earth Vids.

<///JJ_HYND>

"I'm not sure..." I trail off, still debating the benefits of an internal spiral, comfort eating or a strategic cry.

"All is good." He quirks an eyebrow at me suggestively. "I am *Kipid*."

"I...," I pause, struggling for an argument that doesn't make me sound as desperate as I am. My gaze flicks around the room, pausing on the small desktop holo-Christmas tree beside the screen. I come up blank. Nothing but my parents disappointed faces dancing in my mind.

"Fine. Let's do this."

I thrust out my hand to shake on it. He frowns down at it before reaching to hold my index finger.

"Close enough." I roll my eyes and shake my hand at him.

CHAPTER TWO
7 Sleeps til Christmas

Barely a week until Christmas and Callisto's commercial district barely acknowledges the festive season. Not like back home.

I walk along the promenade, taking in the handful of festive signage decorating the storefronts. Festive bunting trails between stores and temporary stalls. People mingle about, and there's a chill in the air mimicking winter.

Up ahead I clock the 'Best hot chocolate in Sol System' street cart. A fully clad being in an environmental suit hands a steaming cup of cocoa to an elven woman with dancing iridescent tattoos on her forehead. I inhale the cloud of chocolate and peppermint as I pass them.

It tastes like nostalgia.

I pick up the pace, bobbing and weaving between the crowds. Multicoloured Christmas lights wind like vines around the tall evergreen trees that line the pedestrian walkways. An unintentional homage to the season when design choices lean towards function over form. Festive merriment a happy bonus to their carbon dioxide scrubbing abilities.

I skirt past a family of four, all with deliberately gaudy matching jumpers. It's nice to see humans embracing the season.

<//MERRY&BRIGHT>

The only thing missing is the smell of burning coals and a man flogging roast chestnuts out of a make-shift cart on the corner.

Decorations aside, it *feels* like Christmas, all the way down to the crowds and frantic shoppers. I have on my crochet Christmas cardigan, a pocket full of festive smut on my eReader, and in a few days my parents will be dancing drunkenly beneath the Christmas tree with an excessive amount of PDA for pensioners.

But before they get here, I need to sort my shit out. Last night Quercus pinged my Glass.

Meet at the Mainframe. 2100 EST.

After that, sleep escaped me and I spent the whole night wondering who my mystery beau might be. *Another Detective Inspector? Human? Male or female?*

I suppose I did specify *boy*friend. Appropriate viable offspring producing partner—keep the parents happy and optimistic about my prospects.

Right, let's do this.

I bypass the masses; veering left at the next junction. The street entrance is bustling as I weave my way forward. I palm the print reader at the gates, push past the turnstile, and I'm in.

The Pleasure District. Adults Only.

And straight ahead... *The Mainframe.*

Okay, time to go get a boyfriend.

The entryway is quiet, calm, like the eye before the storm. Vibrations tremble underfoot from the music currently muffled by the glass doors ahead.

My shoes squeak with each step, and I bite my cheek trying my best to ignore them. I should have worn heels, but I'd rather survive the night without a broken ankle... or two.

<///JJ_HYND>

As I step forward into the den of sin, the sounds of revelry and the clamour of inebriated patrons climb to an overloud volume. The irritating squeaking from my shoes slowly fades.

To my right is the bar, a long counter that stretches onwards *ad infinitum*. Simple, vibrant Christmas lights hang along the back wall nestled among the shelves of wine bottles, spirits, and the like.

It's not *quite* an Earth Christmas. There's a distinct lack of hanging wreaths and snow topped fir trees, and I doubt they'll be pulling out the eggnog or Buck's Fizz anytime soon. But it is nice to see a festive touch here and there, catering to us humans.

A racrurian bumps against my arm as she hurries towards the bar. "My apologies," my *RenChip* translates.

I give them my best, least awkward, tight-lipped smile. "No worries." But they're already gone, three people deep, in a queue for the bar.

I take a deep breath before I gaze around looking for Quercus.

The Mainframe *is* Callisto nightlife.

Where denizens come looking for a good time. It has a reputation for *enabling*. Alcohol. Substances. Gambling. Sex. You want it; *the Mainframe* has it.

And yet, despite its *somewhat* seedy connotations (by human standards anyway), it's all above board. Carefully monitored, heavily regulated, and *very, very safe*. The safest place in *District 2* with a crime rate of **0.91**.

Urgh. I need to kick the work-mode brain for a moment. *Relax, Ali, you might even enjoy yourself.*

<//MERRY&BRIGHT>

A group of beautiful individuals cross in front of me. Short skirts and legs for days. Even the men have their sculpted abs on show... And then there's *me*.

I tug at my tartan mini skirt, willing it to materialise a few more inches of fabric. *Why did I wear this thing?* At least the thigh-length crochet cardigan provides adequate coverage.

The godlike creatures before me saunter past the row of curved booths with shiny stainless-steel tables that run parallel to the bar. The booths work as a barrier to the dropped dancefloor with its pulsating lights and undulating dancers—not a single crochet cardigan in sight, I think as I clutch at the hem of mine, or a festive jumper. More like a sea of skin-tight leather and iridescent sequins.

I tug at my tartan skirt again. I was slimmer when I bought it. All the long work hours, noodle pots three meals a day, and lower gravity have made me soft. Soft and curvaceous.

It doesn't bother me; at least it didn't until I tried on something other than scrubs and a lab coat. Or until I thought someone might see me naked...

Just a fake boyfriend, I remind myself.

"Wow!" a voice calls out, dragging my anxious mind from the inner turmoil and back into the present.

I turn to face Inspector Julia Clark—Quercus' human partner. She eyes me up as her brown ponytail swishes behind her. She's all business in her leather jacket, denim, and boots.

Quercus reclines back against the bar beside her, giving me an approximation of a wolf whistle, before hastily turning back to his partner. "Did I apply that correctly?"

<///JJ_HYND>

"Close enough," She smiles, "You look great, Ali." She sizes me up and then raises an arm at the bald blue gentleman behind the bar, offering three fingers. "Although some liquid courage never hurt anyone."

I feel my whole body clench. Exposed. My skirt climbs higher up my thighs the more I move about. I want to wrap my crochet cardigan around me and go find a cosy corner where I can read.

"I am a bit..." I begin, searching for the appropriate word.

"Rusty?" Julia offers.

I nod. "Out of practice."

Out of my depth, more like.

"Don't worry, I know Varios."

"He's good peoples," Quercus cuts in as he reaches for the drinks. Three small tumblers filled a few finger widths deep with golden syrup. He hands one to Julia and me before claiming the last as his own.

Varios. So that's to be my pretend beau.

"To first pages," Quercus exclaims as he thrusts his drink in the air between the three of us. The 's' in 'pages' struggles to escape around his fangs as he sounds it out.

Julia rolls her eyes and knocks her glass against his, "He means new beginnings. He's trying to learn Earth Standard." She peers back at him, eyes sparkling.

For the first time since I spoke with my parents... I feel, *okay?* The realisation takes me by surprise. No longer nervous, more excited to see where the night takes me. I mean, it's all fake anyway; I might as well enjoy myself.

I exhale a laugh, knocking my glass against theirs, and take a big gulp of the golden fluid. It's sweet, viscous, and glides down my throat like honey. All the way down to pool

<///MERRY&BRIGHT>

in my tummy with the warmth of a hug on a cold winter morning. The warmth spreads, slowly unwinding all the tension as it permeates through me. My shoulders relax first, then my hand unclenches by my side.

"He is here." Quercus jumps up from his reclined position against the bar, and the jostling motion knocks over my glass. The golden wetness seeps through my cardigan— which took me four months to crochet all the squares for and is most definitely not machine washable.

He continues unaware, weaving his way between dancers and bar patrons towards the entrance where half a dozen individuals linger.

"Sorry, the big guys aren't always aware they're so..." Julia starts dabbing at my wet cardigan with napkins from the bar.

"Big?"

"Precisely." She keeps dabbing away.

My eyes are drawn over to the entrance. To the people loitering there.

Who will it be? Which one is Varios?

The name sounds exotic. Let's disregard the three humans who are already far too inebriated to warrant entering a drinking establishment.

There is a gorgeous woman with shoulder-length platinum blonde hair and iridescent lines dancing along her uncovered forearms, but I don't think Quercus is aware I'm bisexual.

The muscular, purple-skinned gentlemen leaning against the entry wall might be the best pick. As he turns, I see his white-out eyes. All pure white from iris to sclera. I vaguely recognise him from the police station's front-of-house community desk. I can't recall his name though. His

<///JJ_HYND>

mouth pulls up into a closed-lip smile as someone waves him over. *Not him then.*

"Here," I turn back to Julia, who has her leather jacket held out to me. "Let's swap."

I shrug off my sodden cardigan—the pockets are the perfect size to fit my eReader, but I swallow down my lamentations, not keen to admit I brought reading material to a date. *Fake date.*

I throw on her leather jacket in time for a throat to clear behind us.

"L-E, this is Varios." I turn just in time to watch Quercus dramatically gesture towards all of me. "Varios, meet L-E."

"It's Ali," Julia corrects.

Varios is staring. His head slightly cocks to the side like a dog might when responding to their owner's voice. "Well met, Ah-lee."

He's covered from head-to-toe in black motorcycle gear. The dark leather clad to his trim form. He looks athletic, in a practical sort of way. Slender legs and wider shoulders, like those Olympic divers.

He's handsome in an odd type of way. Not that attraction matters much in this situation. He has two legs, two arms, and one head. Nothing that will scare off my parents for their first close-up extraterrestrial encounter.

My eyes pause their assessment once I reach his face.

"Hello, Varios."

He takes a deep inhale at my words. *Peculiar.*

He's rather flat faced, with no protruding nose at all. No hair either; completely hairless and smooth. No

<///MERRY&BRIGHT>

eyebrows. No beard. No creepy moustache—that one is definitely a plus.

The rest of his pale face is mostly covered. Thick goggles, that wouldn't be out of place in a steampunk convention, cover his eyes. A cowl covers the rest of his head, and a peculiar bulging scarf wraps around his throat, secured in place with a small buckle.

I don't know *what he is*. I've never met a member of his species before. I've never met any other species before last year though, so that's no surprise. I wonder what he knows about humans. *I wonder if we're compatible.*

My eyes linger on his lips as I picture myself reaching across to touch his face, stroking along his jaw; curious how the pale flesh might feel beneath my fingertips. *Will it be soft like velvet, or smooth like scales?*

Varios smiles at me; it feels forced. His cheeks rise up as he bares his teeth. A mouthful of jagged, pointed tips elicit a gasp from me. Like a shark, he snaps his mouth shut again. He's a predator and his continuing stares have me feeling like prey.

Quercus smiles like a cat that got the cream beside us. "Is good, yes?" he exclaims, "I am *Kipid*." The final word doesn't translate.

Julia hit his arm. "Yeah, yeah, Cupid. Let's leave the two lovebirds to it." She lifts my cardigan slightly, "We'll see you in the morning,"

I nod, waving them off. I take a slow calming inhale before I turn to Varios.

He looks *concerned*. His whole body language screams discomfort.

I gesture at the empty booth nearby. "Shall we?"

<////JJ_HYND>

He unzips he leather jacket revealing a tight-fitting black t-shirt beneath, before he lowers himself into the booth.

Another deep breath. I psych myself up before I join him, dropping into the seat on the opposite side. The noise of the bar dims as the booth's pod-like shape keeps the external noises at bay and amplifies our own voices far more clearly than I anticipated.

He twists to watch Quercus and Julia leave.

This was a mistake. No one will agree to this insanity.

"I'm sorry," I say, "Could you wait ten minutes before you leave?" *Spare me some embarrassment.*

Varios rests one forearm on the table; up close his anatomical peculiarities are more obvious. His oversized hands are bare. The skin is pale. So very pale, bordering on translucent. I can see his blue veins trace along his palm. Small membranes web between each of his three fingers and one thumb.

"Why would I leave?" he asks, his voice low, calm.

"This wasn't what you expected. I'm not..."

His head cocks to the side again as if sizing me up. There's something in his body language that leaves me flustered.

"Not, what?" He prompts.

I clear my throat, "What you expected?" I drop my tone as if it's a secret, "I'm human."

"I am aware." His head tilts to the side slightly, and I picture his eyes inside his goggles gliding over me as he takes me in.

"And you're...." I find myself gesturing to his face before I can stop myself.

"Lumosis." he states.

<//MERRY&BRIGHT>

"Of course..."

I've never heard of them, and I feel rude for not knowing. My cheeks heat as a shift in my seat.

"Well, I won't hold it against you if you want to leave now. A blind date in this day and age? Silly of me to think this would work. We probably aren't even compatible..." I ramble on, my inner thoughts spiralling out of my mouth like verbal diarrhoea.

He reaches forward and places one enormous, webbed hand on my bare skin. His skin is cool to the touch, like a cool flannel on a hot day. The flesh is soft, softer than expected. The sensation quiets my brain.

"We are compatible."

"I... sorry?"

"Quercus told me you require a partner to accompany you to a Flora Festivity. Is this correct?" My *RenChip* struggles, slow to translate the last few words.

"My parents are visiting for Christmas. It's an Earth Celebration. They think I have a boyfriend..." I trail off, wondering if I sound as pathetic to him as I do to myself.

"Why would they think that?" His voice is a balm to my nerves, deep and calming.

"Well, I may have told them that."

"You lied."

"No. Not a lie... Just an infinitesimally small falsehood, so they wouldn't worry." Voicing it aloud makes me sound even more ridiculous.

"Why would your lack of partner concern them?"

Ouch... "Well, I suffer with the tragic affliction of forever-alone-ness," I laugh awkwardly, "My parents want me to be happy. To settle down before..."

"Before what?"

<////JJ_HYND>

"Before it's too late." I shuffle my feet beneath the table, cringing as a single squeak of my shoes sounds off.

I clear my throat. "I'm too old."

He laughs; the sound is loud and abrupt. "You are not old."

"Before I become undesirable," I argue.

"You are a pleasant human to look upon."

"Thank you." Is he *flirting* with me? It's hard to tell with those thick goggles covering his eyes. *Who am I kidding I wouldn't know flirting if it hit me in the face like a wet fish.*

"Before I hit menopause...?" Even I can hear the wavering in my tone. I'm quickly running out of excuses.

"I am capable of producing viable offspring," he states matter of factly.

"Yes. I... Beg you pardon?"

"In case your parents request such information."

"I see..." I pause for a moment. "You realise this would be a fake?"

"It would be false?" His head cocks to the side again.

"We would be pretending." I smile nervously.

"Lying."

"No! Acting. For my parents' benefit," I add.

"So that they no longer have concerns for your lack of offspring."

I sigh. "Pretty much, yeah."

"I see. Okay. I shall help you lie to your parents."

I beam up at him across the table. His thin lips falter for a moment before he smiles back, a little less forced than previously. Smaller, but more genuine, and still showing a little of those razor-sharp predator teeth.

Now that I'm past the initial shock, it's really not so odd. Not as concerning as my first observations led me to

<///MERRY&BRIGHT>

believe. I doubt the anatomy differences would change anything; we could hold hands, or hug. *We could still kiss.*

Not that we will be doing any kissing.

Absolutely not.

"Thank you."

"You are most welcome, Ah-lee."

That's the second time he's said my name, and the first non-human to come anywhere close to pronouncing it correctly. It makes my smile stretch even bigger.

I have a boyfriend for Christmas.

A *fake* boyfriend.

CHAPTER THREE
6 Sleeps til Christmas

"We need to prepare." I pace the length of Varios' office, turning to march back towards his workstation once more. Movement helps keep the nervous energy at bay.

Varios lifts the sheets of multiple-choice questions I had translated for him up from his workstation. I don't need digital records of my desperation. "Will your parents interrogate us?"

"Not exactly... They will ask *questions*."

"Questions," he repeats.

I lift my hand in the air, counting the questions off my fingers. "How did we meet? Where? When? Why? We will need to sound *convincing*..." I ponder a plausible meet-cute as I continue to pace.

"I set up your workstation for you."

"No, that's a bit mundane." I wave my hand as if to shoo away the idea.

"Eighteen cycles ago. Your Glass wouldn't connect to your workstation. I reset it for you."

I stare at him as he fiddles with the papers.

I was surprised to hear he worked at Precinct Two—inside Callisto Police HQ. More so to hear that his office is directly below the forensics lab—my lab. But to hear that we've met before? I'm both shocked and appalled at myself for not recalling it sooner.

<//MERRY&BRIGHT>

'Too busy with your head in a microscope whilst the rest of the world passes you by,' my mother's words come to me.

"I don't remember that." *Why don't I remember that? Remember him...*

"I believe you spilled noodles on your workstation another time, too."

A memory of someone fixing my workstation comes to mind; the recall is sluggish and try as I might, I can't form an image of the individual.

"All is well. Many do not recall their interactions with computer support."

"No, that's not okay. I should remember *you*."

"All is well."

Our eyes meet; at least I think they do. I stare at him through his goggles. I am so absolutely appalled with my past self for treating him like he's the help and not a colleague.

"Your parents will ask all these questions?" he asks, breaking our one-sided staring contest.

I nod fervently. "Oh, absolutely."

"Educational history." He looks up at me. "I studied fifteen rotations on electronics and computing on my home world. You wouldn't know the university."

I nod, borderline psychopathically. Very good, dad will love the commitment.

"And you?" Varios asks.

"Oh, classic Oxbridge story. Nothing exciting."

"I see." He looks down at the paper again. "Extracurriculars."

<////JJ_HYND>

"Sports, creative endeavours, that sort of thing." I sit back on the desk, crossing my ankles together as I wait for his answer.

"I enjoyed long swims with my friends. We would explore the reefs and shoreline caves."

That sounds adventurous, and fun, and it shows my answer right up.

"I studied. I was in the chess club and the homework club. Oh, I loved reading. I still do!" I lift my eReader aloft from my pocket to show him.

He rests his arms on his workstation. "What type of books do you find pleasurable?"

I gulp at the translation of his words. "Fantasy, adventures set on far off worlds; anything with a little spice."

"Spice?"

"Romance," I hastily correct myself.

He smiles at me. "Sounds pleasant."

Returning his attention to the questionnaire, he reads aloud, his forehead wrinkling. "What are your professional prospects?"

I roll my eyes, picturing my dad asking exactly that. "My dad will ask about money. Don't answer him. He's nosey and..."

"I have nothing to hide."

"Not the point. If he asks, just say you're comfortable."

"I am comfortable. I am seated."

"No." A small giggle escapes me. "Financially comfortable. It doesn't matter."

"Ah. He wishes to know if I can provide for a mate. That his offspring shall be taken care of."

<//MERRY&BRIGHT>

Something about the phrase 'taken care of' has my mind take a deep dive off a cliff into a vortex of smutty scenes from my favourite books.

Heat races up my throat into my cheeks. "Something like that." I fight to clear my throat and my mind of the battery of sensual images.

"Are you married?" he reads aloud, his forehead wrinkling.

It's hard to tell where he is looking with the goggles, but I find myself a little self-conscious under his stare.

"If I was married, why would I agree to be your mate?" he says offended.

"I meant previously married."

"I have no mate."

"Okay, moving on..." I clear my throat and continue my pacing again. Concentrate on legs moving; stop brain spiralling.

"Do you?" he asks.

"Do I what?"

"Have a previous mate?"

"I... No. I was never married." I quickly answer, embarrassed by my lack of *anything* outside of my career.

Varios makes a peculiar noise in his throat. A remark on my career driven life, perhaps? *I'm sorry we weren't all swanning about in oceans having fun*, I huff to myself. It's so hard to gauge the meaning, especially when I can barely see him.

I drop my hands in my lap. "Must you always wear those goggles?" I ask.

A moment after his translator explains my words, his hand shoots up to protectively caress the edge of his eyewear.

<///JJ_HYND>

"I have a sensitivity," he pauses. "Do they cause you distress?"

"No, it's fine I..." I look up at him. "Actually, I would like to see your eyes. See your face. To know who it is I am talking to."

He stands abruptly from behind the workstation, heading towards the door.

"I'm sorry, don't leave. It's not—"

He palms the door's control pad. Manually locking it. "Computer, set light to low." He unclasps his goggles—leaving them to hang in one hand—before he slowly turns to me.

"Oh," I breathe out. It's all I can say. All I can think to utter.

He is *ethereal*.

His slim face with its gently sloping features is all very understated, but his eyes are beautiful. He blinks, the double lids sliding open and close in both directions, with skin so pale and translucent, I can almost see his eyes through them. Shiny gunmetal grey, sparkling like two freshly polished grey pearls.

"The light can hurt," he says, blinking as he watches me slowly.

I step forward, pushing myself closer. A warm hue pulses from beneath his skin. In the low-level light, it's more noticeable. Mesmerising.

I lean closer, on my tiptoes, reaching up to his cheek.

"You're glowing." It's all I can think of saying, and yet, it doesn't feel right.

My fingertips almost brush against his skin. He makes an anguished noise in his throat before stepping back,

<///MERRY&BRIGHT>

forcing some distance between us. He quickly reapplies his goggles and returns to his seat behind his workstation.

"Computer, lights to full."

I blink, startled by the sudden starkness of the bright light.

He picks up the fake relationship revision papers once more. "Will you live together before marriage?" he reads aloud. "This is not allowed?"

It takes me a moment to recover myself from what felt like the most intimate moment I've had with another being in a long time. Concerned I made a mistake, a societal faux pas. That I might have offended him, but he's right back to business.

I clear my throat. "It's just frowned upon by some. My parents can be a bit *traditional*."

He nods in affirmation before returning to the papers again.

"What's this?" He points to the last page.

I lean across, one palm resting on the desktop.

"Oh, it's important information about you. If you can fill it in, so I may study it. In case my parents ask."

"Birthday. Favourite colour. Favourite food..."

"Yes, your personal preferences and that sort of thing."

"Wouldn't it be better if we show each other?"

I look up from the paper on his desk, noticing he still hasn't started filling out the preferences section.   "What did you have in mind?"

"I can show you my favourite place. Tomorrow? 20:00. Commercial district."

"It's a date," I say.

<////JJ_HYND>

His lips turn up in a smile, a genuine one with a small slip of sharp teeth. His cheeks raise too, and I wonder how his eyes might have lit up; if only I could see them beneath those thick goggles.

CHAPTER FOUR
5 Sleeps til Christmas

19:38. *Fuck. Still early.*

I'm not trying to be early, but I already walked around my residential block twice to waste time. I walked past the carolers singing *'Old King Wally something...'* enough times they started to recognise me. I push my Glass back into the depths of my handbag.

I don't know *what* the plan is. I don't know *where* Varios is taking me. Which means I didn't know what to wear.

After what felt like hours, I finally decided on a sun dress, with my well-loved loafers and a crochet cardigan thrown over the top. But not until I had already excavated my wardrobe fully on to my bed, twice.

The clear Perspex doors of the lift slide apart, welcoming me to *'the strip'*. I step out into the hustle and bustle. A row of shops ahead of me boast *'best noodles in the universe'*, *'Pickles from Mars'* and *'genuine celery from Earth'*. Pfft, yeah sure. There isn't even *celery* celery on Earth.

Each new proclamation slightly more grandiose—and unbelievable—than the last.

However, I happen to know that Callisto's best noodles are in fact from the little street vendor on the corner by the fountains.

<///JJ_HYND>

My eyes seek out the fountains blasting water fifteen metres in the air, lights tinting them a festive red. The geysers reach up past the balconies of the upper floors, stretching onwards in an attempt to kiss the stars.

They don't of course. They couldn't possibly. The exo-glass domed ceiling prevents that and protects us from the battery of space debris that likes to frequent our little moon.

My eyes drag down to the base of the fountains and a little to the left, in front of my favourite little street vendor's cart, is Varios. Apparently apprehensively early too.

He's not in all-black leather this time. Today he's got his goggles on and neck covering buckled, but below the neck he has on an oversized flannel shirt rolled up to his elbows—it shows off his toned arms nicely and the two small fins that fold out from his forearms. He also sports paint-marked jeans, which seem so alien with what I have come to associate him with.

He turns to face me as if he could sense my presence, waving one webbed hand as he strolls towards me.

"Ah-lee." He smiles with his pointy tooth grin. "Have you hunger?"

My stomach growls as if on cue, and that pulls a laugh from us both.

"This is Marty." He leads me over to the noodle street food stand.

"Evening, Ali," Marty starts, the little bell on his Santa hat jingling. "What'll it be? The usual?"

"Oh, erm..."

"Two *The Usuals*, please," Varios says.

<///MERRY&BRIGHT>

Marty shakes his head with a chuckle as he dishes up two portions of chicken noodles in a black bean sauce. "Coming right up."

"I didn't know you liked noodles," I say to Varios as Marty hands me a noodle box and a set of chopsticks.

"I don't know if I like noodles. This shall be my first attempt." He mimics my actions of pulling apart the wooden chopsticks and rubbing them together to sand away any errant splinters.

"I thought we were showing each other places we liked?" I smile, watching him like a fish out of water. He twists the sticks inside the box, swirling it round and struggling to balance the dripping noodles as he carefully pushes it into his overwide open mouth.

"Correct. This is *your* favourite food."

"How did you...?" I begin.

He struggles with his second swirl of noodles poised on the end of his chopsticks, whilst I slurp at mine. "Noodles were made to be slurped."

"Slurped?" His smooth forehead wrinkles.

"Like this." I grab another wad of noodles between my chopsticks and slurp them up, savouring the taste as the spice makes my tongue tingle. "It's a sign of respect to the chef."

"I see..." He ponders a moment before mimicking my slurps.

"They hurt my tongue." He hisses out a breath between his teeth.

"That will be the chilli." I giggle as I watch him try to fan cool air onto his tongue.

"Not cold, but hot."

<///JJ_HYND>

My lips turn up in a smile, involuntarily. "Yep. So, what's the verdict?" We continue walking along the main promenade bordering the fountains. The small fir trees wrapped in multicoloured Christmas lights have had additional baubles added to their low hanging branches.

"The noodles are adequate."

A chuckle bursts out of me. "Such a glowing review."

"They are edible." He coughs before taking another mouthful.

"Seems like it," I giggle again. "You never answered me. How did you know about the noodles?"

He looks at me over his noodle box. "Your desk is covered in them."

Oh. "Well, that's embarrassing."

"You work too hard." He smiles down at me.

We continue walking past the other shoppers. A section of the main plaza is cordoned off with holo-tape as they set up market stalls. A racrurian in a Santa coat carries a stack of boxes over to the nearest stall; the holo-tape blinking in and out of existence as he breaches it.

"A Christmas market!" I turn to Varios. "My parents will eat this up. They love Christmas."

"Then we should have them attend." He frowns, concerned. "I don't believe human digestion can process... this." He gestures at the iridescent glass baubles being unloaded onto one of the stalls' counter tops.

I laugh. "I shall be sure to tell them."

"Have you completed your noodles?"

I nod. "Thank you."

He takes the empty boxes and places them in one of the public waste bins.

"Where next?" I ask.

<///MERRY&BRIGHT>

He reaches to hold my hand. "Allow me?"

Warmth blossoms inside me at his gentleness, slowly permeating outwards. I place my hand in his as he gently pulls me along beside him, leading me across the crowds mingling along the plaza to the row of storefronts.

His steps halt beside me. "We have arrived." He smiles, looking up at the store signage in front of us.

"Cosmic Scythe," I read aloud.

"Come." His whole being vibrates with energy; excitement rolls off him in waves as he gently squeezes my hand and pulls me after him.

"Welcome to Cosmic Scythe. How fares the weary traveller?" A bespectacled young man with long greasy hair tells me.

Varios leans in conspiratorially. "That means welcome."

"What is this place?" I frown at the young man whose shirt carries an odd brown splodge and a name badge that reads James T.

"What is this place...?" The man scoffs before looking up over the counter at us. "Varios," James T greets, "and who's your friend?" He turns to me, forcing himself to stand a little taller.

"Greetings James. This is Ah-lee," He introduces me, and why does the sound of that make my heart skip a beat? He's gently holding my hand, almost like a caress, and keeping me close to his side. "She wishes to pick a form."

"No problemo, my man." James shuffles from behind the counter, leading us further into the shop. We pass rows of stainless-steel tables and chairs sitting empty for now. One large table is round, and a hologram

<////JJ_HYND>

protrudes from the surface, as if to mimic a planet's terrain. Mountains, valleys, cliffs cresting with oceanic views.

The store gets tighter the further inside we go. Screens line the walls filled with cinematic ads of board games, card games, digital dice sets, other paraphernalia I don't recognise and something I do—books. Real life, bona fide books, with pages.

Further along there is a long counter filled with yet more holograms—a sorcerer, a hunter complete with bow, some kind of warrior complete with creepy little undead minions, and on the far end, a squad of soldiers in exo-suits and excessively large laser guns as if they are compensating for their miniature size.

Finally, the room opens up a little. Three oversized machines complete with glass-fronted doors inset into the wall. They look like replicators, but older. Much older, and definitely not food-grade.

"Here you go, Ali." James hands me an oversized Glass. "We have everything except green, and the succubus torso prints funky."

"Oh, erm... Thank you." I flick through the Glass, swiping side to side. Screens full of body parts—muscular arms, digitigrade legs, full feathered wings, reptilian heads, bikini clad torsos, full plate armour. An endless selection.

"Here." James hands Varios a second Glass to peruse.

"With thanks, my friend."

I find myself less concerned with the catalogue and more enamoured with watching Varios' graceful fingers glide across the Glass.

When his finger pauses, I realise he's looking at me. His head angles down at me, watching. The attention causes my cheeks to heat, so I quickly pull my eyes away and back

<//MERRY&BRIGHT>

to the catalogue. I swipe a few more pages before I land on something cute.

"This one," I say, turning the Glass to Varios.

He clicks on my selection and sends it to print. The wall of machinery begins to rumble. Printer one illuminates. Inside the small window, I see robotic arms descend, crafting my chosen figure from some kind of plastic.

First the feet, clad in cute little boots. Then a wide flared skirt, raising up to the little witch's floral corset top with a cape at the back. She poses with a wooden staff in her tiny fingers. The printer hums, building layer after layer of the model, all the way up past her shoulder length hair to the very tips of her teeny cat ears.

"Aww," I squeal with my face pressed up close to the window. "She's adorable."

I turn to see Various with a peculiar wrinkle on his forehead and his head cocked to one side as he watches me curiously. "Yes. Adorable."

The printer's lights flash for a moment, before the door slides open. My tiny little feline-eared alchemist is complete.

I reach inside, carefully plucking her from the printer's base plate. The residual warmth from the machinery lingering on the little figure in my hands.

"Now what?" I ask.

"We paint," Varios replies easily as he retrieves his own model from the second printer.

<////JJ_HYND>

"Like this." I follow Varios' movements, mimicking them carefully.

I dip the paintbrush again, tapping it against the palettes green. It morphs the brush tip from cherry-red into a forest-green. I use it to apply green stems to the floral details of my little feline-girl's embroidered corset.

As I paint, my brain quiets. Either from the rhythmic dance of our paintbrushes across the figures, or from the steady warmth of Varios thigh beside mine beneath the table. Our legs separated by mere centimetres.

I find myself imagining a world for her, wondering what her life might be like. Does she live in a tower, books lining every wall? Her cat ears flicking as she listens to the log fire crackle, pawing her way through another alchemy book.

"Your mind is busy." Varios' smooth deep voice breaks through my thoughts. "You are frowning."

"Oh." I stretch back in my seat, only now aware how much I was shrimping over the table. My back protests the movement. "I was imagining what type of world Elsbeth might live in."

"Elsbeth?"

I raise up my little half-painted figurine. "I think she'd be a librarian or an alchemist. What do you think?"

"That is the appeal of Cosmic Scythe."

"Imagining a life of unlimited books?" I say.

<///MERRY&BRIGHT>

He laughs; a deep belly laugh that takes him by surprise. The sight of it forces a giggle out of me too.

"That you can live any life," he laughs again, "Is that your wish for life?"

"Unlimited books?" I nod emphatically. "Oh yeah. They're so hard to find. Physical books I mean. I've not found a single store on Callisto that sells them."

"I was not aware they were." He points to the holo display behind us—a book rotating on its pedestal.

"I was very surprised to see them here," I laugh, "What about your figure?"

Varios lifts his small figure up, rotating so I can see it clearly. It's a small human barbarian, complete with fur braces, leather boots, and wielding a great sword in its tiny hands. I raise my eyebrows at its detailed chest, long braided brown hair and miniscule loin cloth... although fur bikini might be more accurate.

If I tilt my head a little, it kind of looks like me, if I was a Xena warrior type.

"Is that what you wish for?" I ask.

"Adventure? Yes. I did. Once."

"No human fetish then," I joke.

He coughs, almost choking.

"Sorry, it was a joke."

He clears his throat, smiling weakly. It showcases just the very tips of his needle-sharp teeth. *I had almost forgotten how very different he is to me.*

"Just a joke," I repeat.

A rumbling vibration tickles my ankle through my handbag on the floor. I grab it, rummaging through the chaos until I can pluck my Glass from one of the inner pockets. The screen pulses green.

<///JJ_HYND>

"My parents," I tell Varios.

Can't wait to see you, Darling!
Our shuttle lands tomorrow.
Kisses, Mum

Fuuuuuck.

I feel the tension returning, all the more noticeable after the relaxing evening we've been having.

"Their shuttle lands tomorrow," I sigh.

"Are we adequately prepared for the hounds?" Varios asks.

I chuckle, alleviating a fraction of the tension building in my shoulders. "Only one way to find out."

A pause lingers between us, uncomfortably.

"Should I accompany you to meet with your parents?" Varios asks.

"I...."

It's on the tip of my tongue to say no. I don't need help. I will figure it out on my own; I always do. But isn't this why we are here?

I swallow down my misplaced pride. "Yes, please. I think a fake boyfriend would help me pick my parents up from the Transport Hub."

A frown flickers over Varios face for a moment before he smiles, his sharp white teeth on show. "Of course, my... Ah-lee."

"Until tomorrow, Varios."

CHAPTER FIVE
4 Sleeps til Christmas

"Ding-dong. Merrily on high—"

"Fuck."

I take it all back. The first set of carollers was endearing, festive and nostalgic. Standing in the doorway to the Transport Hub, shaking mini credit collection terminals as people try to enter is *not*.

I force past the choir, making a beeline for the arrivals hall. The screens flicker overhead. Transports. Companies. Times. Destinations. All flickering over, and over.

Got it.

SolGlider: Earth to Callisto 1145.

The Transport Hub's main screen declares **1137**. I made it with a few moments to spare.

My mind shifts to Varios. *Where is he...?*

I spin around, searching for my handsome, leather-clad alien. No sight of him yet.

A *GravBike* speeds up the ramp from outside, slowing to a halt by the edge of the platforms just a few metres away.

I watch as graceful, long legs climb off the bike and strong arms that reach up to remove their helmet—like a scene from a movie, when the heart throb makes it in the nick of time to the *TransHub* to win back the love of their life. And just like in the movies, the move grabs me hook,

<///JJ_HYND>

line and sinker. I'm practically salivating over the athletic body, watching his firm arms flex.

"Ah-Lee." Varios smiles at me, tucking his helmet under his arm as he steps towards me.

Oh, that walking heart throb is here for *me*.

He leans into me, his face merely millimetres from mine before he pauses. "May I?"

"Yes." I don't know what he's asking permission for, but I want it like—

He caresses his large hand along my cheek before gently grasping my chin between two fingers, and my mind blanks.

His breath fans out over my lips as I inhale the taste of him—salty like a sea-breeze. Holding me still, he gently presses his thin, soft lips against mine for a moment. My eyes flutter closed before he pulls away.

"Did I perform adequately?" he asks.

My face heats, my whole body feels a warmth spreading through it like a wildfire. My voice croaks as I attempt to speak. I clear it before trying again.

"Very adequate," I murmur; my hands instinctively raising to touch my own lips and feel where his touch left its mark.

"Human mates do this."

It's not a question, but I answer anyway, my mind rebooting to its default analytical self. "They do. Yes. With tongues usually."

Where the fuck did that come from? Why did I say that?

His eyebrows raise at my words. "Next time."

Next time...

<//MERRY&BRIGHT>

My mind conjures all kinds of filthy, inappropriate images of Varios and his tongue and—

God, he looks hot. Complex thought fails me. All I can think is hot, sexy and hot. Hot and sexy, and oh my...

He leans back against his bike. It balances perfectly upright, slightly giving from his weight.

"Next time we should—"

"Alison! Darling!" Mum's voice calls out, obnoxiously loud over the noise of the crowd.

I quickly turn from Varios to see her waving at me, oblivious to the other shuttle passengers attempting to disembark. Meanwhile, Dad struggles with three oversized suitcases. At least one too many for one man alone to contend with.

Varios leans over my shoulder, his big body warm against my back, his breath hot against my ear. "I wish for you to continue that sentence later."

The brush of his breath over my ear sends a shiver down my spine. Heat reignites inside me; something clenches deep down.

"Mum," I choke out. "Let me—"

"Darling, what's wrong? You look positively flustered." She begins fussing with my hair, brushing strands behind my ear. "You're warm. Rupert, feel her forehead. She's warm, isn't she?"

I bat her paws away as Dad struggles up to us with the luggage trolley. Varios takes the reins, pushing the trolley effortlessly along the Transport Hub platform.

"Good fellow," Dad declares with a forced handshake. He grasps Varios' large, gloved hand in his. Varios looks over to me confused. "On Earth we shake, Son. Like this. That's it."

<///JJ_HYND>

Varios frowns for a moment before a small smile pulls up at his lips.

"Whoa... You've got quite a set of gnashers on you." Dad, undeterred, continues to beam up at Varios whilst vigorously shaking his hand.

"Dad!"

"Rupert! Don't be uncouth." Mum swats at him.

"Ouch! What?" He gnashes his own teeth together. "Mine are fake. I lament; it's been *donks* since I had the pleasure of nice bit of steak... Speaking of: I'm absolutely famished."

"Rupert!" Mum swats him again.

"What? We've been trapped in that tin can for days!"

"28 hours," Mum corrects.

"And we've barely eaten."

"There was a three-course dinner yesterday."

"Yes. *Salad.* Bloody rabbit food." He rolls his eyes.

"And a cooked breakfast this morning," Mum reminds him.

"Ah, yes. Lovely eggs Benedict. Perfect yolk," Dad reminisces. "What about you...?" Dad gestures.

"This is Varios," I introduce him, "Varios, meet Mum and Dad."

"Right. Big strapping lad like yourself, you must be starved too?" Dad beams up at Varios who turns to me helplessly.

"Have you hunger, Ah-lee?" Varios asks.

I smile up at him. "Sure, let's eat."

<//MERRY&BRIGHT>

"... children are a must. We aren't getting any younger, Son," Dad yammers on to Varios from the couch.

"Our species are physically compatible," he states simply, before he takes another bite of the left-over sushi from lunch.

"That's the spirit, lad." Dad pats his shoulder. "The more the merrier."

"Oh?" My already reddening cheeks are on fire. Scorching. *These two are getting way to comfortable with each other. Too much, too soon.*

I move towards Varios, grasping his arm to pull him down to me. "You know this how...?" I hiss between my teeth, chastising myself the moment the words leave my lips.

"Not personally." He shifts beside me, fidgeting with his left hand—expanding and closing the webbing between his three fingers. He lowers his voice, "There are videos." He rubs his hand along the bulging leather strap buckled around his neck.

Is he nervous?

"I see..." I breathe out at last. "You've... seen..." *Porn, he's watched porn. Of humans....*

"I think that's the last of it, kids," Mum calls out. Varios and I shift apart like naughty school kids caught red-handed. He rubs the nape of his neck as I fidget with the hem of my skirt.

<///JJ_HYND>

Mum bats my hand gently. "Terrible habit, Darling."

"Thank you for your help with the luggage, *Vah-roosh*," Mum attempts. "We shall see you tomorrow, Dear."

"Tomorrow?" Varios and I speak at the same time.

"For the Christmas tree. Look around, Dear. You don't expect to celebrate Christmas like this, do you?" She gestures at the bare living room.

My eyes glide over my domicile. The factory white walls and default furniture. Eight months went fast, and I never got around to doing much with the place. *Hell, I've still got one last box waiting to be unpacked tucked in the back of the wardrobe.*

"She has a point, Darling," Dad chimes in.

"Of course. We need a tree." I say, whilst shaking my head. "And some Christmas lights," I gesture at the bare walls.

"And mulled wine?" Mum asks.

"I'm more of a scotch man, myself," Dad adds.

"I shall return tomorrow," Varios states. "With mulled wine."

"And scotch—Ouch!"

"Don't be uncouth, Rupert."

"I will see you out," I announce, more to keep my nosey parents at bay.

"Goodbye, Dear," says Mum.

"Until tomorrow, lad," says Dad.

Varios takes my hand in his, leading me along the small entryway towards the door, until we are out of direct line of sight of my parents.

He pulls my hand up to his mouth and kisses my palm gently as though it is the most precious thing he has ever held.

<///MERRY&BRIGHT>

I feel my face flush with heat. My heart skips a beat. My insides clench in anticipation. I swallow thickly.

He brushes his other hand over one of my cheeks. "I enjoy your appearance when you pinken."

"I... erm... Thank you," I stammer, embarrassed, flattered—and slightly horny.

"Goodnight, *my mate*."

CHAPTER SIX
3 Sleeps til Christmas

Sixteen, seventeen, eighteen. I trace the panels along the ceiling with my eyes. Eighteen one way, and twenty the other. Almost a perfect square if not for the wall of built-in storage.

The wall pulses with a soft warm hue; a visual cue that morning is breaking. Never mind Callisto doesn't have proper mornings like we do back on Earth. The warm light spreads through the room like a sunrise, alerting me to the start of a new day. I didn't sleep for more than a few fitful hours, but morning waits for no one.

I thrust over the covers, willing myself the energy to start the day.

The door slides open; footsteps make their way over to my bed. "Alison, Good morning."

"Mum?"

"Oh good. You're alone."

"You burst in here, even though you thought I would have company?" I ask, slumping back onto the bed. The absolute *joy* of having parents under the same roof again.

"No." She waves her hand at me dismissively. "No, your father worried."

"At least one of you did," I mutter under my breath.

"Anyhoo... Darling, what's the plan for today?" she asks.

<//MERRY&BRIGHT>

I groan as I cover my face with my arm. "I have work. You must entertain yourself until I get back."

"And how long will that take?" She pouts like a petulant child.

"After lunch. I took half a day," I say. "Perhaps you and Dad could take a walk around the promenade, get some breakfast, and I'll be home for lunch."

"And festive fun."

"Yes, festive fun."

"And don't forget the Christmas tree."

"Yes, Mum."

Work goes about as well as expected. The mythical night workers have left me yet another stack of work leftover from the night before. Luckily, it's not much, as the human half of Callisto negotiated reduced holiday hours starting tomorrow, and it seems everyone's been tidying up to get ahead of themselves.

Time passes slowly. Too slowly.

Nothing new comes in.

No Inspectors appear to darken my doorway.

It's almost **1300**, and I'm about to shut down my workstation when the door pulsates with light.

"Computer, open door."

Inspector Julia walks in, complete with a festive shirt beneath her leather jacket and my crochet cardigan over one arm. "Thought you might want this back." She places it neatly on the edge of my desk.

"Thank you." I rub my hand over the fabric, the familiarity of it soothing.

"So...?" She asks.

"So?" I parrot as I check over my cardigan for signs of a stain from the drink mishap.

"Come on." She slumps down into the chair opposite, a mimic of her partner Quercus a week ago. "How's it *going*? With *Varios*?"

A smile plays at my lips, involuntarily.

"That well, eh?" she smirks.

"No. Nothing happened."

Her eyebrows raise. "That's exactly what they all say, right before they spill the beans."

"He's different than I expected," I say.

"Too different?" She raises an eyebrow at me, and I can't help but think she means much more than her words. "Listen, it's none of my business, but Varios is a good guy. He's helped us out big time in the past. He is kind and loyal to a fault."

"It's just pretend, remember?"

She slaps her thighs. "Right, well, I'm overstepping."

"Not at all. Thanks, Julia." She nods at my words. "And for returning this," I say as I caress my precious crocheted masterpiece.

"I washed it."

My eyes flare wide as I process her words. I clutch the fabric, praying it hasn't shrunk.

"Dry clean only. Don't worry, I know what's up."

Thank fuck. "Thank you, I appreciate it." I breathe a sigh of relief.

<//MERRY&BRIGHT>

"Quitting time," she states as she leaves. She pauses at the door, turning back to me. "Varios really is a good guy. Maybe give him a chance." She holds her hands up in mock defeat. "Okay, okay. I'm done overstepping. I'm going."

I smile. "Merry Christmas, Julia."

"Merry Christmas, you filthy animal." She winks at me.

I chuckle, turning back to my work. I finalise the last chemical analysis data set before shutting down my workstation, slide this morning's noodle box into the bin, grab my freshly returned crochet cardigan, and I'm out of here.

I can't help the smile that curves my lips. I'll never admit it to them, but it is nice to have my parents here. I am looking forward to decorating, to drinking mulled wine, and to Dad snoring through Christmas vids after one too many glasses of scotch. I'm excited, perhaps a little too excited to see one person in particular.

I take it all back; my parents are intolerable Christmas fascists.

"What's this?" Dad dangles an emaciated string of tinsel between his fingers.

"The best I could do on short notice," I sigh.

"Darling, I hate to be pessimistic—"

<///JJ_HYND>

The room's lights pulsate, alerting me to someone at the door.

"Hold that thought," I call out as I speed over to the entrance. *Talk about being saved by the bell.*

My fluffy socks glide the last metre as I struggle to balance before I reach the door. It glides open with a hiss of cool air from outside.

An arm shoots out to steady me.

"Whoa, thanks." My eyes climb up past the tie and scarf, further still to gaze into goggles. The polarised tint reflecting my own brown eyes back at me.

"Varios," I breathe.

"Your socks lack sufficient friction," Varios states, as he frowns down at me with concern.

"Hi," I say, breathless.

I would be lying to myself if I said I hadn't missed him in the time we'd been apart.

"Greetings."

"My parents will be excited your here."

His smile falters, causing mine to as well. "Of course." He turns to leave but pauses mid-step. "Scotch is human drink, correct?"

"Yes..." I start before I hear the telltale jingle of glass bottles clinking together.

"Is that Varios?" Mum shouts from the living room.

"Correct," Varios calls out to her.

"There you are lad. I'm outnumbered by women." Dad walks along the entryway towards us.   "Well, let the poor boy in from the cold." Dad shoos me aside.

"This is for you, *Roo-purr*." Varios offers a bottle of single malt to my father.

<//MERRY&BRIGHT>

"I knew I liked you." Dad grins from ear to ear, his hands grasping the bottle. "Darling, Look! Varios brought the good stuff."

"You didn't have to." I smile up at him. "That was very thoughtful." I can feel my heart warm, butterflies dancing in the low of my tummy. Julia was right; Varios is kind. A gentleman.

"I have something for you also." He drops his backpack to the side; I can see greenery poking out from the top.

"Oh... it's a...?"

He hands me a potted fruit tree. A handful of small oranges hang low in its small branches. Tiny green leaves cover them and nestled amongst it all—dozens of small silk ribbons in deep greens and ruby reds are tied to the branches.

"For your festivities," he says.

I hold the round terracotta pot in both hands. My mind whirrs to connect the dots. "It's lovely," I say, my head tilting to examine the beautiful plant, but failing to understand why he'd gift me one.

"Winter Flora," he states, smiling down at me.

"Oh." Oh. *Oh*! "It's a Christmas tree?"

"Quercus told me orange is a festive fruit... You don't like it." He reaches for the plant in my hand.

I pull my hands back. "No. I do. It's very thoughtful. I'm surprised you could find an Earth fruit tree on Callisto." I smile, leading him into the living room.

"It was no easy task."

"Pardon the chaos, Darling," Mum says as she removes a cardboard box of baubles from the walkway.

<///JJ_HYND>

Empty boxes litter the ground, discarded in Mum's efforts to round up as many festive baubles as possible. Dad cautiously navigates the room to find a clean glass in the kitchen, pouring himself two fingers of scotch.

"Any ice?" He asks.

"No."

"Ah well, when needs must." He collapses down into one of the dining chairs around the glass table.

"What's that you're holding, Dear?" Mum asks as she rummages through another box of supposed festive cheer.

"A Christmas tree. Varios gifted it to me," I say. She pauses for a moment, staring at the small orange tree blankly. "How, kind," she says before throwing herself back into the rummage.

Varios moves towards the Christmas chaos in the middle of the living room, pausing to inspect a few branches of the faux pine tree taking centre stage. "This is the naked tree we must clothe?" he asks, turning to me, his head tilting in that way that's becoming increasingly endearing to me.

"That's right. But not with actual clothes. With this stuff," I say as I lift a bauble from one of the boxes and swish gold tinsel his way.

The rooms lights pulse again.

"What now?" I frown.

"Oh, that's for me, Dear," Mum calls out in her singsong voice, "Varoosh, be a dear."

He looks at me, forehead wrinkled, before Mum pulls him after her.

"Thank you, Darling." There's a clamour of noises from the hallway. "And these ones."

"What are you—"

Varios rounds the corner, arms laden with boxes.

"What on Earth...?" I start.

Mum taps my chin to close my mouth. "You'll catch flies like that."

Varios places the boxes beside the tree, passing the first box over to my mother by the couch.

She reaches inside and plucks out a candy cane bauble. I march over to the boxes, plucking out a feathery robin on a clip.

"What is all this?" I demand.

"Decorations, Dear."

"I can see that..." I huff. "Where did you get them?"

"JiffyDrone."

"Oh, like the advert," Dad chimes in excitedly.

"I didn't know they delivered Christmas decorations," I say accusatorily.

"JiffyDrone. We'll be with you in a jiffy," Dad sings.

"Mum?" I prompt.

"They do if you tip nicely." She plucks the robin from my fingers and clips it to the tree. "There, our first decoration."

I feel the spread of Varios' warm fingers against my lower back. "Why is there an avian on the winter tree?"

"It's a winter bird." I shrug. "Honestly, I don't know why half of this stuff is Christmassy." I lift another bauble from the box, this one a small red pick-up truck from the early 21st century—it even has tyres!

"Tradition, darling." Dad raises his glass in the air.

"Speaking of tradition." Mum points above me.

I knock my head back to stare at the ceiling; directly above my head hangs a small sprig of mistletoe.

"More Flora?" Varios asks, his head just beside mine.

<////JJ_HYND>

"Technically it's poison," my analytic brain regurgitates.

"Poison?" Varios looks down at me alarmed.

"It means we have to kiss," I almost whisper.

He leans in, one hand beneath my chin to arch it up at him. "Gladly."

Our lips brush; his mouth presses against mine softly. The words '*next time*' ring in my mind. *Fuck it.*

I glide my tongue against his closed mouth; he freezes momentarily, lips parting slightly in surprise. I push my tongue between them; he reacts hesitantly at first as his tongue tentatively touches mine.

I glide my tongue against his, savouring the sensation, enjoying the slight salty taste of him. He tilts my head, pressing his lips tighter to mine as he pushes into my mouth to dance with my tongue. I find myself leaning into it, into *him*. The warmth of his chest is against mine. His big hands cup around my back, holding me against him.

I gently suck on the tip of his tongue, and he groans loud enough for me to return to my senses a little. *We have an audience.*

I pull away breathless; he reluctantly releases me. I step back, turning back to the mostly bare Christmas tree.

Heat rises in my cheeks. I clear my throat. "Shall we?"

"Once Varios recovers," Dad chuckles to himself.

"I think you broke him, Dear," Mum adds.

I turn back to Varios. He has a peculiar expression on his face—a single frown line between his brow bones—and one hand caresses his lips as if reliving the touch of mine.

"Varios?" I ask softly. "Everything okay?"

<//MERRY&BRIGHT>

"Yes, *my mate.* All is well." He reaches for my hand and pulls me close again. "I wish to take you on a date."

"How romantic," Mum singsongs.

I blush. "Of course. How about we finish this tree first?" I joke awkwardly.

"Tomorrow evening."

I smile. *Why does this feel like he wants something real? A real date, with real feelings.*

"Don't leave him hanging, Darling!" Dad shouts.

I nod, smiling up at Varios. "That would be lovely."

"Huzza!" Dad calls out.

Mum rolls her eyes at him. "Now, this tree won't dress itself, Darlings.

Lights pulse around the room.

"Is that—" Dad starts.

"Don't wait up," I announce loudly as I rush past them, leaving them both nursing cups of steaming mulled wine on the couch. I hurtle towards the front door, slipping my feet into boots before I palm the door controls.

"Hi!" I breathe out as my domicile's door hums closed behind me.

Varios stands before me in his tight black motorbike leathers, helmet tucked under one arm. He momentarily freezes at my abrupt entrance.

I brush a strand of hair behind my ear, shrinking under his unwavering gaze. "Is there something on my face?" I laugh awkwardly.

"No. You are beautiful."

"Thank you, Varios." I pull at the hem of my dress; the soft, green velvet smooth between my finger and thumb. *Mum's right, this is a nervous habit I need to kick.*

He pauses again, before jerking back to life.

"Apologies, let me take this." He reaches for my handbag and stows it away in the back of his bike.

"I've never ridden one of these before."

He pulls out a spare helmet and leather jacket—human sized and pale pink in colour. "I shall be your teacher."

<///MERRY&BRIGHT>

Heat blooms inside me. I clench my thighs together. Swallowing to clear my drying throat. *How did he make that sound so erotic?*

He lifts the pink helmet over my head, pausing. "May I?"

I nod. He peers down at me; his warm salty breath brushes against my lips. If I took a breath right now, I would taste him.

He brings the helmet down over my head, pushing it into place. "All is well?"

I nod again and he knocks down the visor, shielding me from the fluorescent overhead lights along the street.

"Where are we going?" I ask.

"Winter lights." He smiles before donning his own helmet.

Taking my hand, he leads me to the back of the GravBike. His voice is muffled by the cushioning of the helmet against my ears. "Winter lights are festive, correct?" he asks, his head tilting slightly in that way I've come to interpret as curious or quizzical.

"Christmas lights? Oh, yes. Very merry." I pause to watch the muscles in his arms flex as he settles me in the front of the bike.

Then he gracefully throws one leg over the back and climbs on behind me. The bike gently dips under his weight. I can feel the warmth from his chest as he shifts into place; the heat of him permeates through my back.   He leans forward; his strong arms wrap around me as he reaches for the handlebars.

His deep voice rumbles, "Ready?"

I nod, despite the nervous flutters low in my stomach. I clench my toes inside my boots, grip the seat

<////JJ_HYND>

beneath me, and say a little prayer. Though, if tonight is my last, at least I get to experience being in the arms of a smoking hot alien. I swallow thickly; glad the helmet and visor hide the pink tint my cheeks have almost certainly taken on.

"Let's go," I call out.

Varios flicks a switch and the bike hums to life. The engine lights up, pulsing crimson, and the bike lifts against the drag of gravity.

He gently grips at the throttle, and we head off down the street. Gently at first, past the residents chatting and shoppers walking home together arms laden with gifts. Until we hit the motorway.

Varios shifts from lane to lane, skimming past taxis, and goods transports. Little else is out here.

Over my shoulder I watch as the district's city centre fades. The built-up commercial zone on top of the residential zone, on top of industrial zones; it all fades into a blur—a single oversized skyscraper reaching up to pierce the exo-dome's roof.

The cool air catches in my throat with each breath, but my body burns as bright as a thousand torches. I am hyper-aware of every centimetre of Varios' body connecting with mine—even despite the leather between us. Each rise and fall of his chest and each flex of his strong thighs beside mine.

I don't catch what he says, my mind completely consumed with watching him move, but as he speaks, his chest rumbles against my back.

I face forward again and see *it*.

Nothing but black concrete onwards to the horizon and framing it are a thousand stars twinkling bright. Giant

<///MERRY&BRIGHT>

balls of gas, burning brightly millions of light years away, leaving a sparkle in the otherwise black void of the sky.

"Breathtaking," I sigh. "You know, usually the light pollution of the district centre is too bright it blocks out the stars—"

Varios' deep voice is against my ear. "Out here I watch the stars and think of you."

"Of me…?"

"Every night."

"I—" The words stick in my throat.

I love that, and I hate that I love it. That a boyfriend of convenience can stir any kind of emotion inside me is concerning. Lust is one thing, and easily ignored, but the tempest of butterflies low in my stomach raises all new complications.

I don't want the warm and fuzzies. This is transactional… At least I thought it was. It was meant to be.

The engine of the bike hums low as we gently slow, turning down another lane. This one small and sheltered by trees—real life Earth trees. A sycamore, an oak, a cherry-blossom—Wait. Work. The data analysis. I should make a note of this.

As I look up over my shoulder to see Varios gazing down at me, my mind empties of everything but him.

I'm totally fucked.

He leads the bike onwards as we reach rows of large houses with neat green lawns and white picket fences. Slowing to a steady pace, the bike's engine thrums quietly.

"We have arrived," he declares as he takes a left on Sycamore Cresent.

"Wow…" My mouth drops open at the sight.

<///JJ_HYND>

This is Callisto Suburbia, where the retired rich of Earth come to live away their final years.

The houses are ten metres tall, with decorative wooden beams, huge floor to ceiling length windows and enormous double carved wooden doors—they look antique—a mimic of a bygone era. Manors, or stately homes might be more apt, line both sides of the wide road.

Big long ropes of Christmas lights cover the houses, following the rise and fall of the roof awnings. Some flashing, others still. One large house on the left has faux icicles dripping along its large bay windows, glowing a cold white.

The manors sit in a neat line, leading along to culminate in a cul-de-sac.

In the centre is a patch of grass with a huge fir tree erected in the middle. It's decorated with thousands of tiny warm lights, ribbons and baubles, and beneath it are enormous, wrapped gift boxes.

"This is incredible!"

"I had hoped you would find the winter tree pleasant."

"How did you know this was here?" I shout, the sounds a little loud as the engine cuts out and we drift to a halt.

"Julia told me." He climbs off the bike gracefully before offering me a hand. "I thought it would bring you pleasure to witness."

I place my smaller hand in his much larger one. "Thank you."

He gently pulls off my helmet. "You are most welcome." The cool air hits me, and I wrap my scarf tighter around my neck.

<//MERRY&BRIGHT>

He rests my helmet on the bike before he pulls his off, and beneath his helmet he's bare. No goggles. His eyes gaze down at me, and a soft pale hue glows beneath his skin.

Before I realise what I'm doing, I push up on to my tiptoes and gently kiss him on the lips. He blinks in surprise.

"Oh, did I misread this..." I pull back slightly, embarrassed.

"Absolutely not." He wraps his arms around me, holding me tight to his chest as he kisses me back. Harder and deeper. Our tongues dance together; he tastes like a sea breeze.

I push myself closer, tighter; my teeth nip at his bottom lip causing him to moan against my mouth that sends a lightning bolt of desire through me. I clench my thighs together desperately, craving the friction.

We pull apart, breathless.

"You are very skilled at kissing," Varios compliments as he brushes a stray hair behind my ear.

"And you're a fast learner," I laugh.

"I have the best teacher," he purrs as he leans closer again to kiss me. Gently this time, placing his soft lips against mine.

He winds his long fingers through mine, resting his forehead against me. Closing his eyes, his hot breath fans across my cheek. "I require a moment."

"Okay," I reply, equally breathless. My mind finally quiet. The pulse between my thighs now a gentle thrum. My body responds to his, even just soft gentle touches. *My knickers are going to be drenched by the end of this.*

I twitch, rubbing against him. He groans.

<////JJ_HYND>

"Ah-lee, I lose bodily control when you are in close proximity," he breathes.

A smile pulls at my lips.

I'm happy, for once I am actually fucking happy about something, anything, outside of research, or work, or some academic achievement.

I'm standing in the middle of the street surrounded by Christmas decorations and beautiful houses. I have an incredibly hot guy who seems to be totally into me. This seems like a dream, like a cheesy romance vid. We're just missing snow.

And I am so *fucking* horny right now. That kiss was a tease, one I'm not ready to end.

"Then don't," I whisper.

He opens his eyes, gazing down at me.

"Then don't control yourself," I say, bolder. "Tell me what you want."

His eyes shoot to my mouth, then up to my eyes again.

"I can show you." He reaches for me, pausing before he touches me. "May I?"

Goosebumps prickle my skin; a shiver chases along my spine in anticipation. "Please," I breathe.

His big hands grab my waist, lifting me with ease. My legs instinctively wrap about him. His mouth takes mine, hungrily. I sigh against his lips; the warmth of his body against mine is bliss.

Desperate for more, I run my hands along his chest. Hungry for more of him, to know him. My fingers clutch at the waist band of his leather pants, and he groans. He groans at *my* touch, at the *thought* of *my* touch beneath the fabric.

<///MERRY&BRIGHT>

Hard metal brushes against my back before he perches me on the leather seat of his bike, releasing me to adjust himself through his pants. And fuck, does that bulge look monstrous.

I don't know what it looks like, but I've never wanted anything more.

He pushes me back gently. I lean on my elbows, and he drops to his knees before me.

"What are you...?"

The obscene bulge in his pants fights against the leather. His sleeves squeeze at his biceps as he shifts.

"Allow me to worship you." His head tilts.

"Right here?" I ask, breathless.

"Everywhere."

"Yes." As if anyone in their right mind would ever say no to this alien god of a man. And he wants to worship *me*.

"I—fuck." Air rushes out of me as his big hands palm my thighs and pull down my tights. I cringe as I watch my red knickers with gingerbread men dancing hit my ankles— the least sexy pair I own.

"I have dreamed of this." His cool breath fans over my bare pussy.

"Of fucking a human?" I ask. My mind is reeling; his breath tickles my sensitive skin.

He frowns at me briefly. He holds my chin and stares into my eyes, into my soul. "I have dreamed of tasting you and bringing you pleasure so that I may witness you writhe beneath me."

"Oh." I can't breathe, I can't think. My pussy is pulsing, and Niagara Falls is about to start streaming down my inner thighs. I don't know what to say; my brain has ceased working. I whimper, "Please."

<////JJ_HYND>

"Gladly."

His head is beneath my dress in seconds; his tongue glides along my folds, sparking pleasure.

He leisurely laps up my juices. "Mmm," he hums.

I fidget in my seat, self-consciousness rearing its ugly head. *What if I taste odd? What if I look strange to him? What if he doesn't like—*

"Fucking fuck," I gasp as he gently sucks my clit into his mouth, rubbing his tongue over it in little circles.

"Pleasant?" His deep laugh rumbles against my pussy.

"Fuck, yes," I groan as his tongue sweeps over my clit once more.

"Tell me how I make you climax," he breathes against my sensitive skin.

"Here." I lick two of my fingers before I run them through my folds, dipping inside.

Proving he's a quick study, Varios gently places one finger inside me. It's much thicker than mine, and I gasp at the pressure of being gently filled. With gentle strokes, in and out, he explores me. Tracing circles around and around my clit with the tip of his tongue, whilst he gently eases in another finger. Only two fingers and yet, I feel the slight pressure of being filled. I push forward, grinding against his face and fingers.

"Oh, fuck," I hiss out, "Right there."

"Here?" he mumbles against my sensitive flesh.

"Don't you dare stop."

I sense a crescendo building, pressure deep inside me waiting to be released. Begging for it.

Varios swirls his fingers inside me, rubbing deliciously against my bundle of nerves. My thighs tremble, warring with the need to clamp together.

<///MERRY&BRIGHT>

"You're going to make me come," I groan, my head falling back.

"I hope so," I can hear the smirk in his tone.

My whole body tingles, my oversensitive flesh is on fire, and I'm one small touch away from exploding.

Varios fingers curl inside me, his fingers rubbing as my pussy clenches around him.

The dam opens, and my orgasm rips through me. Waves of pleasure as Varios continues to finger me, and suck at my clit.

"Oh fuck!" I crush his face into my pussy, grinding it against him. The pleasure continues, each new wave bringing me closer to a second orgasm.

My pussy slurps at his fingers greedily, and then I'm done. I come again with a loud moan, and something else releases deep inside me. A gush of juices spurts out of me, into Varios' face and he laps them up like a man starved.

I bite my lip to hold in my groans of pleasure as I slowly come down from the high. It's been so long since I last came, I thought my body had forgotten how.

His wide hot tongue licks me clean, before he gently redresses me pulling my gingerbread man knickers back up into place.

My legs are like jelly as he pulls me into his arms, kissing me gently as he strokes my hair. He runs his tongue along my lips until I part them; his tongue darts inside to play with mine. The taste of my pussy lingers on his tongue. We pull apart, breathless once more.

"You taste exceptional." He smiles, resting his forehead against mine.

<////JJ_HYND>

"Thank you," I mumble, too boneless to be self-conscious. "A girl could get used to this every night," I muse to myself.

"Gladly."

I gaze up at him, wide-eyed. "Next time."

He smirks back at me. "Until then, allow me to return you home."

CHAPTER EIGHT
Christmas Eve

Last night's date replays in my mind, repeatedly. The lines of fake and real are blurring. My analytical mind likes to compartmentalise life into neat little boxes. Work. Family. Home. This is something else, and the warm and fuzzies keep growing, spreading like bacterium in a petri dish.

I pull my pillow over my head; perhaps if I lie here long enough, the world will right itself and everyone can forget the past week happened.

"Alison!" Mum's shrill voice calls out.

Yeah, no luck forgetting she exists.

"What time is *Var-oosh* coming over, Darling?"

And no luck they will let me forget the past week either.

"Or is he already here?" Mum stage whispers as she opens the door to my bedroom.

I lift the pillow just enough to watch her fumble about; one hand held out in front of her, reaching about and the other covering her eyes.

"You can drop the theatrics. He isn't here."

"Oh." She drops her hands and makes a bee line for the bed, dropping herself on to the edge before thrusting a steaming mug in my direction.

"Mmm, coffee." I reach for it.

"And *why* isn't your gentleman friend here?"

<////JJ_HYND>

I inhale the steam, taking a sip. Bitterness dances on my tongue, followed by a sharp kick. "What's in this?"

"Oh, your father added a little something." She waves her hand at me, dismissively.

"So, where is he?"

"Who?"

"Who, who... Are you an owl?" she grumbles, "Varoosh, of course."

"He will be here later, Mum."

She leans in conspiratorially, and far too close considering its early morning. "Why isn't he here?"

She thrusts back the covers, revealing my crumpled oversized t shirt and fluffy socks.

"Tut-tut." She jumps up, aghast, heading for the door. "Thank God, I came prepared."

"Prepared?" I grumble, taking another sip of the spiked coffee. Hmm, once you get used to it; it isn't half bad. I won't be telling Dad that, though.

"Mum?" I call out.

"One moment, Darling."

I take another long sip before putting it on the bedside table and dropping my head back on the pillow. My eyes flutter closed.

"Here."

"I was just resting my eyes..." I jolt up to sit again, rubbing away sleep.

"You sound like your father." She rolls her eyes. "Now, take it."

As I open my tired eyes, she holds out a large flat box in her hands.

<//MERRY&BRIGHT>

"It's not Christmas yet," I protest, as I reach for the beautifully wrapped box with red and pink stripes, and a magnificent, oversized bow.

"Yes, well I thought you might need it. For tonight perhaps..." Her words linger in the air between us.

"What?" I pull on the ribbon, and slowly lift the lid, immediately thrusting it down again.

"Mum, what is this?" Heat creeps up my throat.

"Var-oosh is a good boy." She lifts the lid of the box again. "And I want grandbabies."

She lifts the delicate ensemble from the box—its red, delicate and bordering on transparent in parts, with a large, tied ribbon at the front. There's a matching thong that would best fit the description of dental floss.

"He'll love it." She slaps her thighs and begins to stand. "Right, I shall leave you to your coffee."

She saunters over to the door, leaving me to stare at the abomination in my hands. That's an unfair assessment—it is pretty, sexy in fact. On anyone else it'll be gorgeous, but on me? I can already tell it'll be an abomination.

But maybe, just maybe, Varios would like to see it. To see me and to unwrap me, like his own personal present.

"Oh, Darling." Mum hovers by the door, one hand resting on the doorjamb. "Merry Christmas, Alison."

"Merry Christmas, Mum."

Time ticks by so slowly. Pulling out my Glass, I check the time again. **1702**. I watch the two morph into a three. **1703**. It's been exactly one minute since I last checked. No new messages. No new notifications.

Dad squeezes my arm. "He'll be here soon, Darling."

Mum pats the seat beside her on the couch. "Come, watch with us. This is the best part, he's about to get his wings back."

I slump into the couch allowing my body to deflate, melting into the couch cushions. A week ago, I didn't know Varios existed, and now it feels like a part of me is missing whenever we're apart.

I fiddle with the sleeve of my wooly jumper—I had to turn down the climate in here a full ten degrees just to make it tolerable. The sleeve is starting to unravel slightly, but I wouldn't change it for the universe.

I've had it for years. I wore it at Aunt Marge's last Christmas, and her blind old dog Jeffers jumped onto the table for the gammon joint, knocking the gravy boat all over me. It must have taken eight washes to get the smell of beef out. Even now, one of the three reindeers has permanently darker antlers than the other two.

I wonder if Aunt Marge would like Varios, not that it matters as they likely will never meet. The thought sends a ping through my chest. I'll miss him after the holidays.

Where is he? He's meant to be here by now surely. I glance at my Glass again. **1705**.

Dread fills me, fueled by his absence. What if I crossed a line last night? What if he didn't like it, like me? Oh, fuck! I squirted *directly* into his face—I didn't even know my body could do that. I mean of course it's biologically possible for humans, but for me?

<///MERRY&BRIGHT>

He's aquatic though. What's a little moisture? Yeah, it's probably fine. I think. I hope. I—

Light pulses through the room just as I stand to try to shake out my tummy flutters. "I... will get that."

"Okay, Darling."

"Shhh, you're talking through the best part," Dad grumbles.

As I walk to the door, nervous energy twists in my stomach, the tempest growing fiercer with each step.

I palm the door panel, and it slides open with a hiss. Cool air pours in from outside, sending a shiver through me.

"Ah-lee." Varios beams at me excited before quickly embracing me in his arms. He kisses me quickly on the lips, then a second time more softly before he whispers, "I have been lost without you."

A smile pulls at my lips. My hands brush against his strong arms; soft fur beneath my fingertips.

"What are you wearing?"

He takes a step back and drops a large sack by his feet. "I am Mister Christ Mass." He raises his arms to show off his suit. It's red velvet, with a fur trim, paired with his black motorcycle boots and gloves.

"Santa Claus?" I laugh.

"Him too." His smile grows wider, a few of his sharp pointy teeth on display. It's no longer alarming; in fact, it's cute. He's cute. This is adorable and I love...

I swallow thickly.

"*Var-oosh*!" Mum appears behind me. "You're looking very festive, Darling." She grabs his elbow, wrapping his arm around hers. "Come, we have gingerbread and cookies."

<///JJ_HYND>

He grabs the black sack before he allows her to drag him off into the living room.

"Oh, good fun, lad," Dad pats him on the arm before leaning in conspiratorially, "The ladies love a Santa suit at Christmas." Dad winks.

Varios looks back to me, his eyes pausing on my lips for a moment, before Mum thrusts a glass of warm milk in his hand. "Help yourself to a cookie."

I walk behind the couch, removing the glass of milk from Varios. "He can't drink milk Mum; he's not a mammal."

She mutters to herself before offering the plate of cookies to him again. "Eat up. You're a growing boy."

I frown at her.

She stares back, eyes wide, in a silent 'What?' like she's playing innocent and not up to her matchmaking tricks. It didn't work last year with the neighbours son—Fred? Frank? Phil, that was it. He was awful. I guess I got lucky with the whole Jeffers/gravy boat incident as Phil kept a wide berth once I stank of beef OXO.

I round the kitchen counter, heading for the mulled wine simmering away on the heat plate. A nice festive treat to get me in the mood and help calm the nerves.

I hear them nattering on and poor Varios taking it like a champ.

"This one is about a dog finding his way home," Mum says.

"And that one's about fighting off burglars," Dad adds.

"Crime is festive?" Varios asks.

"Hmm, oh and this one he has to stop terrorists."

"Rupert, for the last time it's not a Christmas vid," Mum chastises.

<///MERRY&BRIGHT>

"He's literally wearing a Santa hat, Darling."

"Alison, Dear!" Mum calls. "We're starting the next vid."

"Coming," I grumble into my cup before I take a sip of mulled wine. The spices tingle along my tongue as the warmth works its way through my body. This is the taste of Christmas.

I take a deep breath before stepping back towards the living room. Butterflies flutter in my tummy, and I'm still feeling unsettled about the growing warm and fuzzies I have for Varios. But, considering how he's currently sandwiched between my parents like a hostage, I doubt I'll have a chance to talk to him about it any time soon.

"What are we watching?" I say as I slump into the seat beside Varios, forcing Mum to budge up.

"Hello," he says.

"Hi," I breathe, inhaling his scent. He places one palm on my knee, and my body can't help but respond. Perhaps I'm ovulating, or he's got sexy alien pheromones fueling my hormones. Either way, this is going to be a *long* night.

Dad's snores turn to gurgles as his head drops back against the couch. Mum's eyes flicker open and shut, her head dipping every few minutes before she catches herself.

"Mum?" I gently pat her arm.

<///JJ_HYND>

"I'm not tired, you're tired," she spouts as her eyelids flick open once more.

I roll my eyes. "Sure, but Dad's gone."

"Where's he gone?" She straightens up, glancing over to Dad, loudly snoring with each exhale. Then her gaze falls on Varios and me, and her surprise flicks to cunning before she smiles. She faux yawns, "Ah, is it that late already?"

She stands, stretching dramatically with a large yawn. I narrow my eyes. She's being suspicious.

She slaps Dad on the thigh. "Come Darling, it's past your bedtime."

Dad grumbles to himself as he comes to, slowly rising to follow Mum to the guest room. "Coming Dear."

The door to their bedroom closes with a soft hiss of air and then I wait. A moment. Two more. Thirty seconds pass and silence reigns.

"Finally," I breathe out.

"Do you think they shall return?" Varios asks.

Not if they know what's good for them...

"No. Probably not." I smile.

"Should I leave?" he asks.

I frown, upset. Does he want to leave? Why would he want to leave now that we're finally alone? "Is this because I squirted in your face? I'm sorry about that. I honestly didn't even know I could do that, and—"

His lips collide with mine; his tongue glides along mine as his large palm holds my head close to his.

I run my hand down the firm planes of his chest, following the ridges of muscles down his abdomen. I can't wait to undress him, to feel his soft skin beneath my fingers.

<///MERRY&BRIGHT>

His other hand strokes along my jaw, down my neck, and lower still. His fingers pause, hovering over my breasts. My nipples harden, pricking beneath my jumper. What I would give for him to pinch one, or better yet to pull them into his mouth, sucking and nipping on the tender flesh.

He pulls away, breaking our kiss.

"It would bring me great pleasure if you would kindly spurt your juices in my face again," he says, running a finger over my bottom lip. "I will not leave if you ask me to stay."

"Stay." I reply immediately.

"Gladly."

I climb into his lap, straddling his thighs. The heat of him searing against my pussy as I shamelessly grind myself against him.

He groans, "Ah-lee, what are you...?"

I kiss him gently before pulling his bottom lip into my mouth to nip and suck on it.

"What do you have on under here?" I ask as I toy with the buttons of his Santa jacket, "Can I take a peek?"

"Please," he murmurs. He gazes up at me, his eyes hooded.

I thrust open the red velvet, the buttons popping, to reveal a delicious expanse of flesh. My fingers trail along the pale skin, soft and smooth. Lights dance beneath his translucent skin, the streams following my wandering hands as they travel ever lower. Lower and lower. The lights pulse down in a parallel to spine, all the way beneath his belt line.

I pause at the waistband of the red velvet pants. When I imagined him coming for Christmas, I hadn't anticipated sexy Santa complete with a sack of gifts and a jingling bell with each step he takes.

<///JJ_HYND>

Varios leans up on his elbows. "All is good?" he asks, his thin lips in a concerned line across his slender face.

I lean forward to place my lips against his. He smiles against mine. "This just isn't how I pictured Christmas going," I laugh.

"Nor I," he gasps, swallowing the end of his words as I palm his cock through the red fabric. "It is better."

I rub my fingers along his length, his girth spanning across the width of my palm. I wonder how it'll fit, knowing damn well I'll revel in my body slowly swallowing him whole.

With one hand I push the velvet pants lower; his cock springs forth, the bulbous tip mere inches from my face. A frill of membrane twirls around it from tip to base. The length pulses with light in time with the lights pulsing along his spine.

"Oh," I inhale sharply. "How festive."

He breathes out a harsh breath, as though he has been holding it in. I look up at him, fluttering my lashes as best I can for my approximation of a seductive look.

"It can fit, I've seen."

"Vids?" I tease.

"Yes." He swallows, his eyes pausing on my lips as I slowly edge closer to the bulbous tip of his cock. "You need preparing first." He exhales sharply as I fist his cock with my right hand.

"Do you have a human fetish, Varios?" I ask, leaning back on my legs. I know this is fake, it's *definitely* still fake, even if part of me wishes it wasn't, but even so something inside me needs to know. Did he agree to this because of some cross-species fetish?

<///MERRY&BRIGHT>

He watches me carefully, his eyes following the trail of my tongue as I wet my lips. "No. I have an Ah-lee fetish. *You* are a fascination."

"Fsshtik," he hisses, his eyes fluttering closed. My RenChip doesn't translate profanities, but I understand the sentiment.

"You like that?" I say, blowing cool air over the tip of his cock as I pump my hand up and down his length.

"*Wait,*" he forces out.

I ignore it and continue to pump him with one hand and massage his balls with the other. I lean forward bringing him almost to my lips. Darting my tongue out to run over the small opening in the tip.

"I cannot...." he says as I run my tongue over the small slit once more.

He grabs my braid tugging tightly; the pain pulls at my scalp in the most delicious way that sends pleasure right to the apex of my thighs. I can feel myself getting wetter.

"Stop," he hisses. His balls clench in my hand.

"Are you about to—" Cum spurts into my mouth, spilling out from between my lips to drip down my chin. I swallow instinctively, the taste like salt on a sea breeze.

His head drops back against the couch pillows. One arm raising up to rest on his head, shielding his handsome face from me. I'm not sure when the alien-ness of it shifted in my mind, but he is handsome, in an unconventional way, but it's there.

I look down at my hands; glowing neon green fluid stains my palms and seeps between my fingers. I wipe my chin against the back of my jumper sleeve, and it too comes away glowing.

<////JJ_HYND>

When I peer up at him, he's already watching me. His slim lips turn up into a smile as he takes in the mess of neon cum covering my face.

"Beautiful." He reaches for me, pulling me into his embrace.

"You cum like a glowstick?" I muse aloud.

"Apologies. That should take longer." He rests his arm over his eyes, breathing heavily whilst I rest my head on his chest.

"I'll take that as a compliment then."

He laughs against his arm. "Please do. You are magnificent."

CHAPTER NINE
Christmas Day

I wake slowly, the room gently illuminating in an artificial sunrise just like any other day. Warmth radiates up my back and along my stomach to my chest. A large palm gently rests against my tummy, fingers spread wide, almost protectively. Another hand holds me close, clutching me to the hardness at my back.

"Varios," I whisper.

He pulls me in closer; my back pressed against his chest as he rubs his face into my neck inhaling deeply.

"Well morning, Ah-lee." His voice is husky from sleep.

"Good morning," I whisper back.

I turn to face him, realising a particular hardness that was pressed against my back is now rubbing against my stomach. Heat rises in my cheeks.

"You're still here," I say.

"You thought I should leave?" he asks.

"No. This is nice." I say before groaning, "Sorry, I must have terrible morning breathe." I cover my mouth with my hand. I turn to rise from the bed and deal with the toxic morning breath.

Varios clutches me tight again. "Stay. Allow me to enjoy this longer."

I settle back into bed, resting my head against his warm chest. He sighs beneath me, his long fingers stroking

<///JJ_HYND>

through my hair gently, sending tingles along my skin and a thrum between my thighs. My heart beats like a drum inside my chest. Each stroke, each touch is bliss, and it almost feels like... *love*. *Almost.* Maybe, if this had been real from the start, we might have had a chance together.

"Alison!" As if on cue, Mum's shrill singsong voice calls out. "*Var-oosh*, Darling!"

"Just ignore her," I say as I rub my face into his chest to inhale his scent; sea breeze mixed with a manly musk.

"Father Christmas has been," Dad calls out.

"One more minute," I grumble.

Varios laughs, a deep sound that rumbles through his chest.

"Your parents have little patience." he laughs.

"They will go away if we ignore them."

The door to the bedroom opens, and the smell of bacon and eggs wafts in.

"On second thoughts." My stomach grumbles at the delicious smell.

I look up from Varios' smooth, muscular chest to the door and see Mum wafting her hand over a plate of a full cooked breakfast.

I roll my eyes. "Mum, I have company."

"About time," she smirks. "Now, breakfast is ready, Darlings."

She gives Varios an appreciative look before shooting me a wink.

"Now, make haste before your father eats it all."

"I heard that," he calls from the other room.

"Yes, and I'll hear all about your high cholesterol from the doctor again if you're not careful," she scoffs as she leaves, the door closing gentle behind her.

<///MERRY&BRIGHT>

"Have you hunger?" Varios asks.

I peer up at him to find him already gazing back at me, his grey eyes shining like pearls. I sit up, the covers dropping from us to reveal more of his bare chest; an expanse of very lickable, smooth skin. His muscles bulge as he shifts up on his elbows. One nipple-less pectoral clenching as his reclines. My mouth waters and I find I couldn't care less about breakfast.

"No," I reply, but my body betrays me, my stomach rumbling loudly in protest.

He laughs. "Your body protests."

"I'm not ready for this to be over," I admit.

A moment passes, silence hangs between us, and I worry I've said the wrong thing.

"I care little if your tongue is bad," he says before he holds my chin and leans forward to kiss me.

I press my lips against his. Soft—so soft, and pliable against mine. He works his tongue against mine and my mind reels back to his bike and how he worked my clit so wonderful.

He pulls away leaving me boneless in his grasp, and my mind blanks of anything except this god-like creature before me.

"Let us satiate our hunger," he breathes against my lips, and I am about ready to throw off his pants and ease that giant cock of his inside me. To see just how incredible those frills will rub against my sensitive flesh. I grind my pussy against his thigh, seeking the friction.

He kisses me on the nose. "Come, before your parents search for their offspring again."

<///JJ_HYND>

Oh, he means *that* kind of hunger. Varios has unlocked my libido, and I can't find the switch to knock it off again.

"Fine." I reluctantly pull myself from him to clamber to the edge of the bed. My body protests as his warmth leaves me.

"Goodness Alison, don't you look beautiful," Mum says, "Doesn't she look beautiful, Varios?" She knocks his elbow with her own.

"Captivating," he replies.

Blush creeps up my neck into my cheeks as I bask under his gaze. His head cocking to the side in that way he does when observing it. Suddenly, despite my little red dress with fur trim, I feel exposed beneath Varios' gaze.

Dad emerges from the guest room with red velvet pants and black suspenders. I groan into my hands, "Oh no."

His black boots thud against the floor with each step as he rounds the table towards Mum. He saunters towards her, pinging his suspender, and waggling his eyebrows.

"Darling, save it for later," Mum purrs.

Ew, parents.

Dad paws at her. "Come sit on Santa's lap."

"Gross." I faux gag.

They kiss. It's loud, and obnoxious, and gross.

<//MERRY&BRIGHT>

I clear my throat. "So, what's the plan for today?" I say loudly whilst trying to distract myself by faffing about with my coat and scarf.

"Christmas market," Mum and Dad answer in unison.

"Right, we'd best get going then." I smile up at Varios who follows my lead.

I shift out of the room, escaping the excessive PDA my parents have on display.

Pine trees three metres tall surround the usually bare plaza, enclosing the Christmas market. The babble of voices rise in the air from the crowds. We pass under the sign '*Weihnachtsmarkt*', merging with the hustle and bustle.

Hundreds of small huts fill the space, all in neat parallel lines. Each hut is filled with patrons—shopping, eating, chatting.

Humans and aliens alike stream between the market stalls, the babble of voices rising in the air as the crowds shift from stall to stall.

The smell of meat roasting over an open fire fills the air. We keep walking, weaving through the crowds with Varios' larger body forming a nice barrier from the crowds. He pauses at a stall selling glass baubles of all shapes and sizes. In the back of the hut is a draconian gentleman in leather pants and waist coat, blowing hot flames onto glass

<////JJ_HYND>

as he moulds, pulling and pinching the molten glass into intricate shapes.

"Kids!" Dad shouts over the noise of the crowd, "I've found the good stuff."

Mum wraps her arm with mine, urging me forward to a smaller stall on the very outskirts of the plaza.

Dad greets us with steaming glasses of honey-coloured liquid. "Now get this inside you." He hands one to Varios.

"Hot," I warn him.

Varios gently sips at it. "Mmm, sweet."

"Warm mead." I smile at him, his face lights up as his cheeks rise and his lips pull up in a smile. He has his goggles back on to protect his delicate eyes from all the harsh lights, but now I know him, I can see the subtle changes in his expression.

I take a steaming glass mug from Dad, the warmth seeps into my palms as I take a sip. "Delicious, thanks Dad."

Varios leans in behind me, his hot breath against my ear. "Not as delicious as you."

A shiver chases along my spine, his words sparking flutters between my thighs. I sip at the hot mead.

I flick my eyes back to my parents—that'll keep my libido in check. Dad is practically gyrating against the poor woman, shimmying the opening of his Santa jacket at her, and she is... actually into it. Urgh. I'd faux gag again, but I wouldn't want to waste the mead.

Instead, I glance around hunting for...

"There it is!"

"You found some?" Dad asks, pausing from his teen make out session with my mother.

<///MERRY&BRIGHT>

I grab Varios' hand, waffling my fingers with his long ones. "This way," I say.

Mum and Dad follow us, bringing up the rear.

We weave through the people, following the smell of sugar and spice, and all things nice.

I drag him to a large double hut at the centre of the market.

"What is this?" Varios asks, pointing at the pictures above the hut.

"Waffles." Dad grins.

Mum rolls her eyes. "We can't have one year without bloody waffles?" she sighs.

Dad ignores her. "Four waffles. Two with chocolate and banana," he calls out the server before turning to me, "and one powdered—"

"Powdered sugar." I nod. "What do you want?" I ask Varios.

He points to one of the pictures on the board.

"Strawberries and cream it is," says Dad.

"Four waffles," the server confirms.

Dad nods, tapping his credit chit to the stalls large Glass on the counter.

"Here." He passes down Mums first, followed by mine and Varios'.

I steal a strawberry from his waffle, licking it clean of whipped cream.

"Ah-lee!" he exclaims, in mock outrage.

"I licked it, it's mine now" I laugh.

His eyes darken, his head tilting as he watches my lips clasp around the end of the strawberry.

I swallow thickly; images of how this night might end peeling through my mind.

<///JJ_HYND>

He leans in close again, my parents walking on ahead of us. "Berries make me recall the sweetness of your pink buds. Exceptional."
Fuck.

CHAPTER TEN
Christmas Night

"Well," Mum yawns, "I'm absolutely shattered."

Dad grabs at her backside. "What about a little visit from Santa?" He winks at her, and I resist the urge to faux gag for the third time today.

"Please, not in front of the children," I say.

"Speaking of children, don't you have something to do?" Mum stares at me pointedly, eyebrows raised.

"Do I...?" Oh. *Oh.* Hesitation halts me in place, my mind spiralling at the speed of light. *Does Varios even want...*

I peer up at him watching me with reverent eyes. He wants me—at least in this moment. He might not be mine forever, but he's mine for Christmas, and I plan to make the most of it.

"I do have a final gift for you" I say before leaning close to whisper in his ear. "If you want me?"

He swallows thickly, his Adams apple bobbing in his throat. "Always."

"Night everyone," I say quickly as I drag Varios behind me.

The bedroom door hums closed behind us. I immediately pull of his shirt and thrust my hands under his T-shirt. He inhales quickly at my touch.

"Cold?" I ask.

<///JJ_HYND>

"Unexpected," he replies before grabbing my hips and pushing me against the wall. He kisses me, once, twice; harsh, bruising, desperate kisses as he slides my cardigan over my shoulders.

"Stop."

He halts immediately. Hands dropping to his side.

"Get on the bed."

He drops on the bed in silence, watching me. His eyes flick between my exposed shoulder and my lips.

"Close your eyes."

He instantly clamps them shut.

"Don't open them," I say as I shuffle out of my skirt and into the red abomination my mother gifted me. The soft lace glides up my thighs and into place. I turn to the mirror to adjust the bow, so it covers at least my nipples, as my rounded breasts bulge beneath the red velvet ribbon giving me the mother of all under-boob.

My head tilts as I step back to take myself in. I look... hot. I look hot as fuck and my hands instinctively raise to caress my bosom. My soft plump breasts fill out the material nicely and my nipples harden to create pert, little peaks beneath the fabric.

As I spin back to face the bed, I catch Varios waiting, one fist clenching against the bulge tenting the front of his pants, and the other held firmly against his eyes as if he didn't trust himself not to look.

I tiptoe closer, placing one palm against his chest to guide him back against the bed.

His breath hitches as my fingertips glide across the naked expanse of his chest.

"Huh." I stroke circles over his pectorals. "No nipples," I muse. "I know, I know. You're not mammalian."

<///MERRY&BRIGHT>

"Correct."

"Not sure how I didn't notice it before..." I drift off into thought.

"You were preoccupied." He groans out, and I realise my hips are pressed flush against his, my pussy grinding against the hard outline of him through his pants as I shift about.

I lean forward, peel his hand away from his eyes, and gently brush my lips against his.

"What do you think?" I ask.

"You remain the superior kisser," he smiles against my mouth.

"I meant the outfit."

His eyes flick down between us, his smile morphs to a full-on grin with sharp teeth on display. "You are a gift."

I sit back on my knees straddling him and jiggle my breasts for him. They bob up and down, his eyes following the movement as though magnetised.

"Want to unwrap me?" I tease, sliding one thick velvet strap down over my shoulder.

"Gladly." Varios surges forward, placing his big hands behind my back and holding me to him as he kisses me. The student has surpassed the teacher as his tongue glides along the seam of my lips, waiting for them to part so he can dart inside. He rubs his tongue against mine, twirling them together as his hands clutch me closer. I grind my hips against him, revelling in the friction of his hard member through the fabric.

I reach up to his goggles. "Let's get rid of these." Pulling them away to drop them on the bedside table. His pearl-grey eyes shine as his blinks, his eyes adjusting.

<///JJ_HYND>

"That's better," I say as I stroke my fingers over the planes of his cheeks.

"Do you have sufficient light?" he asks.

My eyes flick around the room, before landing on the cardboard box stashed over to the side. "More light would be good." A mischievous smirk tugs at my lips.

"Stay here," I command and he relaxes against the bed. "Good boy."

I climb off his lap, bending over to rummage in the box. I peer behind me to see his head turn towards me, watching my movements. Shaking my money-maker at him, I grab the string of lights from the box and saunter back towards the bed.

I loop the cable along one side of the headboard, trailing them over to Varios in the centre of the bed. I straddle his chest as I wind them round his wrists—first the left one, then the right, making sure to leave a little wiggle room between them. I do a final loop on the far side of the headboard. I sit back to admire my handiwork.

"Computer, Christmas lights on."

The winding fluorescent LEDs flicker to life, bathing the room in a festive glow of reds, oranges, greens and blues.

"Now I can see." I smile, feeling pretty pleased with myself.

Varios groans, his hips lifting as if instinctive.

I tuck a strand of loose hair behind my ear. "It's not too bright for your eyes, is it?"

"No. All is well," he says, his eyes never straying from my lips.

I lick them, running my tongue across the soft flesh. His hips shift again.

<///MERRY&BRIGHT>

"Ah-lee," he groans.

His brow furrows, his fists clench inside their Christmas bondage.

I lean in close. "Tell me what you need," I whisper.

"You." His hips flex again.

I press my lips against his, teasing him with my tongue running along the seam.

"Like this?" I ask.

He groans into my mouth, and I swallow it greedily.

I reach beneath me to grab his cock. It feels like a steel bar in my grasp. "Or like this?"

He lurches forward, the lights twining around his wrist making him pause.

"Ah-lee, you tease me." His breath hitches with each new clench of my palm around his cock.

The heat of his cock sears through me, my body burning. I rock my hips against his chest, revelling in the friction.

"I'm teasing myself," I moan as pleasure sparks and a particularly harsh grind of my hips has my clit dragging across his abs, pinched between the fabric and his firm muscles.

I could come like this. I clench my thighs together, trying to will away the growing sensation from climaxing too soon.

I shift lower down his body, his cock slapping against my thigh as I go, until I sit hovering just over his hips.

I brush my fingers beneath his waistband, wrapping my cool fingers around his hot cock. He hisses.

"Ah-lee," he pleads.

I thrust down his pants, his thick cock bobs free, lights dancing along its length. My mouth practically waters

<////JJ_HYND>

at the sight. I lick my fingers, gliding them beneath the lacey fabric to swirl across my clit. I push the thong aside leaving my flesh naked to the air.

He instinctively bucks his hips, the large tip drags through my folds, and I bite my lip to swallow my moans.

"Wait," he says but his actions do the opposite as I feel his hard cock drag through my folds again. "We must prepare you."

"Like in your videos?" I tease.

He nods jerkily.

"I think I'm prepared enough," I say before I gentle push my hips down. His bulbous tip nudges against my entrance. I slowly push harder, moisture seeping out of me, dripping down his length.

"So big," I murmur as I start to rock back and forth, easing him inside me.

Pressure builds as I'm slowly stretched wider and wider. The slight pinch of pain, holding me on the cusp of pleasure.

"Taut," Varios forces out. "So taut." His eyes flutter closed.

"You like that?" I murmur as I wiggle back and forth, grinding myself against his cock. My tits bounce with each movement; the ribbon barely containing them rubs against my nipples deliciously. The buds of them tighten into pert little points. I slide down his cock, slowly by surely my body swallowing each delicious, girthy centimetre of him.

Varios nods emphatically. His eyes open to gaze up at me.

"Your body grips mine well."

<///MERRY&BRIGHT>

I feel a slightly prick of pain as I manage to swallow the whole bulbous tip inside me. "Fuck," I breathe as the pain quickly gives way to pleasure.

My inner walls are stretched to bursting. Pressure spreads across my sensitive insides. Juices leak from between our joined bodies to coat my thighs.

"Fuck." It's all my lust addled brain can think to say as I struggle to stay perfectly still, sat on his cock. If I move, I might come and I don't want to. Not yet.

I bite into my bottom lip, clenching my thighs together as my pussy flutters around his cock.

"Oh no," I huff out. "You're going to make me come."

I shift from side to side, my muscles starting to burn, sweat beading on my brow. "I can't hold..."

My pussy clamps down tight, milking the bulbous head buried inside me. My head falls back, my eyelids fluttering half closed as my mouth drops open in an 'o'.

Varios watches me in rapture as the pleasure ebbs and flows in waves. I lose track of time; it could be seconds or hours and I wouldn't know. All I know is that I'm split apart on his cock, stuck in a perpetual state of orgasm, and all other men have been ruined for me.

He leans forward trying to reach me. "Ah-lee?" The frilly membranes along his forearm tickle against my check. I giggle, my insides clenching and Varios groans.

"Well, that was embarrassing," I say. "That usually takes longer." Heat creeps at my cheeks.

"I understand."

I notice his hands fisting the air as if fighting to hold himself still.

"May I?" he asks.

"Please."

<////JJ_HYND>

His hips rise, inching forward slowly. Moisture pools between us, lubricating the way. Slowly I slide down him, swallowing him whole.

"Oh my..." I grind against him instinctively as I feel his frills tickle against my sensitive flesh.

As my body adjusts to take him, he slides in and out more smoothly. His hips bucking faster. As he rises, I grind down to meet him.

"Fstikk," Varios grits out.

He pistons in and out of me, the frills along his shaft swirling, rubbing against that sensitive bundle of nerves deep inside me. I bounce on his cock, my tits escaping their confines as they tumble out of the ribbon. I run my fingers along my body, pausing to pinch and knead my nipples between my fingers and thumb.

"Varios." I twitch against him. "Make me come," I murmur needily.

"Gladly."

He attempts to grab my hips; his wrists still tangled in the Christmas lights. He grunts with frustration as he thrusts into me hard and deep. His frills tickle my insides whilst the bulb on his tip continues to stretch me.

His movements grow jerkier. In and out, in and out. Juddering.

"Ah-lee," he moans my name. "Kiss me."

I lean forward to take his lips with mine, pressing slanted kisses against his mouth. The movement shifts my insides, tightening around his cock like a vice.

"Fsstik," he curses against my mouth. I suck on his tongue, pulling it into my mouth, and he jerks against me. Warmth spills inside me, pressure building as he fills me. I come with a gasp, my pussy clenches tight, continuing to

<///MERRY&BRIGHT>

milk him. His seed spills out around our joined bodies, neon paints down my thighs and his abdomen. He surges forward, halting as the Christmas lights pop behind us.

The room is bathed in darkness once more, with nothing but his bioluminescence glowing from within. The soft hue of it makes him appear ethereal.

"I lo…" I stop myself, biting my tongue. What the fuck am I doing? I can't *say* that. I can't *feel* that. It's *not* real.

I raise myself off him, his cock slides out with a slurp followed by a gush of neon cum. My insides clench around nothing. I feel hollow—bereft.

Varios slips his wrists free of his Christmas light bondage; it dawns on me that he could have done so at any point but he wanted to follow my commands. He chose to remain restrained.

His large palms encircle me, pulling me into his arms. I rest my head on his chest; his heart beats like a drum beneath my ear, his bioluminescence pulsing in time.

"Ah-lee," he murmurs as his long fingers stroke circles along my spine. "Gratitudes."

Why is he thanking me? "I should be thanking you," I joke.

He laughs. "You are most welcome."

He opens his eyes, peering down at me as he blinks slowly.

"Are you well?" he asks.

"Of course," I sigh. My body misses him being inside me already. *Fake dating my arse. I fucked myself over with this.* "Are you?"

His brow furrows for a moment, just a moment and then it's gone. "All is well."

<////JJ_HYND>

The hollowness inside me grows, emotions I can't name crash over me. Unspent tears burn behind my eyes and a lump forms in my throat.

"Should I leave?" he asks.

I glance at the clock on the bedside table. **1205.** "Christmas is over," I say quietly.

His body stiffens beneath me. I sit up clutching the covers to my body.

"I have to take my parents to the TransHub early. They've had a memorable Christmas, I think. Thank you for helping me with this," I waffle on, the words tumbling out like verbal diarrhoea. "We should do it again."

I tag on the last part, leaving it open for him to swoop in a take me up on that offer. To give me a sign that this, any of it, meant even half as much as it meant to me.

"Next winter tree," he says quietly.

I smile weakly. "Next time."

I bite back the tears building behind my eyes. *How can we go back to being strangers after what we just shared?*

CHAPTER ELEVEN
Boxing Day

Warm light radiates across the room in an approximation of a sunrise. The same as every day, the same as yesterday. I turn and throw my hand into the blankets— empty. Empty and cold without him here beside me.

Tears bite at my eyes, and I take a slow breath in to calm my emotions. I knew the warm and fuzzies were growing. I knew I would miss him when it was all over. I didn't expect it to hurt so much. My heart feels cleaved in two.

"Alison," Mums calm voice calls out, the voice she pulls out when she's about to tell you bad news, or there's a looming emergency. That's how you know it's serious.

I roll over with my back against the door, pulling the covers over my head as I sniffle into the pillow.

"Ali, Darling." The bed dips with her weight as she sits beside me, her hand brushing over my shoulder. "Is it as bad as all that?" she asks.

I turn to face her; tears tracking down my cheeks.

"Oh, my little girl." She pulls me up to her, hugging me as she softly rubs my back. The way she did when I was a little girl scared of the dark.

It makes the whole thing worse and tears spill easily now, a sob wracking my chest.

"Did you two have an argument?" she asks.

I shake my head.

<///JJ_HYND>

"Did he hurt you?"

I shake my head again, wiping my cheeks dry on the edge of my sleeve.

"Do I need to call your father in here?" she threatens.

"He would never hurt me," I assure her.

"Then what happened? *Var-oosh* seemed like such a good boy." She smiles patiently.

"It was a sham," I admit, sniffling.

"A sham?"

"Fake."

"Yes, I know the definition of sham." She rolls her eyes. "There was nothing fake about the way that boy looked at you."

I wipe my nose on my sleeve. "Really?"

"I don't know aliens," she starts.

"We try not to call them aliens."

She raises an eyebrow at me. "I don't know non-humanoids, but I do know love. And that boy was head over fins for you."

I giggle, sniffling. "You think?"

"Not a doubt in my mind." She rubs the remaining tears from my cheeks and tucks my hair behind my ears. "So."

"So...?"

Mum rolls her eyes, standing from the bed to rummage through my wardrobe. "So, go get your man back."

"It was fake remember? Our agreement was just for Christmas."

She launches knickers, stockings and a skirt at my head.

<///MERRY&BRIGHT>

"Negotiate new terms, as your father would say."

"Negotiate..." I trail off.

"Alison, this is the first time I have seen you happy and excited about anyone or anything outside of work."

Shame peels through me.

"I love that about you. How driven you are. How important your work is. But if you let this man go without even trying..." she sighs. "Then you're a fool."

She's right.

"You know I'm right."

Annoyingly so. I rub the wet sleeve across my eyes again, jumping up to shuffle my ass into the skirt, pulling my stockings on one at a time. I stand just as mum hands me a Christmas jumper.

"Wait, your shuttle leaves soon," I state as I run my fingers through my hair to brush out the tangles.

"We can sort ourselves out. You go get your man," she smiles at me.

"Thanks Mum."

"Those grandbabies won't make themselves," she calls out as I run out the door.

And there's the mother I know and love.

I step up to his door, the choir up the street marching along oddly close to me. Their singing is like nails

<///JJ_HYND>

on a chalkboard for my nerves. My stomach twist and knots as I stand here waiting outside his door.

"You can do this," I take a deep breath, and tap the console on the door.

I lift up my Glass, setting it to project my handwritten notes above my head.

He opens the door.

'Varios, I wasn't looking for a real boyfriend...' The text scrolls.

"Ah-lee?" His head cocks to the side.
The choir grows louder as they make their way to the next domicile, only two doors behind me.

'It took a fake relationship for me to realise that...'
The glass scrolls.

'You are perfect for me.'

"*Ah-lee*, I cannot read human."

"Oh right..." I drop the Glass from over my head. "I was trying to be romantic." I blush at my foolishness.

"Romantic?" he asks.

"Varios, I know this was meant to be fake. But I can't do this. I don't want it to be over."

"Why didn't you tell me?" Varios asks, his forehead wrinkling.

"It was just pretend, remember?" I say, "I couldn't expect more from you. We had an agreement."

"It was never pretend to me."

"But I'm just a strange looking human."

"I never said you were strange."

No... he's right. He never did. "I..." The words catch in my throat.

He reaches for me, pulling me against his chest as his door closes behind us. Using one finger to lift my chin, he

<///MERRY&BRIGHT>

says, "You are the most incredible, beautiful female I have ever witnessed. With pink lips that beg to be kissed. And eyes that mesmerise far greater than any deep-sea lure every could."

"I..." I can't breathe, can't think. What does this mean?

"What about next Christmas?" I ask quietly.

"If I can only have you for winter tree, then I want them all. Every year."

"What about Easter?"

He frowns. "Another festivity? Yes."

"Halloween?"

He laughs, "That also."

"Thanksgiving? Although that's more of a North American thing, but Aunt Marge loves any excuse for a party," I waffle on. "And fireworks. Loves a good firework display. Jeffers not so much..."

"Ah-lee."

"Yes?" I look up at him from beneath my lashes, tracing the soft lights pulsing beneath his skin.

"Be my mate?" He leans closer.

"For—" Our lips hover closer.

"For always," he breathes against my lips.

"Yes." I kiss him gently and he moans into my mouth.

He drops to his knees before me, resting his forehead against my stomach. "I have hungered for you."

He peers up at me, watching as he slowly glides his palms up my legs. Pausing when my tights give way to flesh, he frowns.

"I'm wearing stockings."

<////JJ_HYND>

He frowns, tugging my skirt until it falls to my ankles, giving way to my knickers and stockings. His fingers trace along the lace tops of each hold up.

"These socks are pleasing," he murmurs as he pushes his face against my knickers. I already know they're going to be drenched, and he groans as he sucks on me through the thin fabric.

He spins me around, my palms against the wall, as he slides my knickers down. Pushing my head down, I arch my back, pressing my butt back into him with my legs spread wide. I shiver at the cool air across my naked pussy.

His mouth hovers millimetres from my bare flesh. His hot breathe sends goosebumps along my skin. "May I?"

"Please," I whimper.

He kisses my hot sensitive skin, before his tongue flicks out tentatively to taste me. He brushes it along my folds, my pussy clenching at the sensation.

His tongue swirls along the seam of my entrance, swirling at the apex where my clit hides. His flat nose brushes against my butt. One large palm holds one hip, the other reaching between my legs to toy with my clit as his licks long stripes across my pussy.

"That feels so good," I murmur, my face pressed against the wall.

Then he surges forward, his thick long tongue entering me. His small nose nudges against my butthole as he tongue-fucks my pussy. In and out, again and again, whilst his fingers swirl circles over my clit. My hips back against him, wildly, involuntarily.

"Fuck," I groan.

With a slurp, he pulls his tongue out to lap up my leaking juices. "Mmm," he moans against my sensitive flesh.

<//MERRY&BRIGHT>

His tongue glides through the wetness, from the very tip to the bottom, continuing until he reaches my butthole. He pauses.

Fuck that. I grind back against his mouth and his tongue dips inside. Gently stretching me open as his thick tongue enters me.

I gasp at the sensation.

My knees quiver, knocking against each other as he continues to rub my clit to oblivion. My eyes roll back inside my head as my body gives into the pleasure. His tongue fucks me harder and deeper and my butthole flutters around it... He moans with each clench; the vibration of it feels delicious.

With one final deep thrust of his tongue inside me, I stretch wide and gush against his hands. Moisture spurting out of me as I come, clenching around his tongue, riding his finger against my clit. Waves of pleasure roll over me; my knees give out as I collapse boneless against the wall. He holds me steady, gently lapping at my moisture.

My mind blanks, and I'm left in a haze, thoroughly sated with my arse in the air and my face pressed against the hallway wall.

"Fuck," I breathe out. "I've never... I've never..." I murmur repeatedly.

"I eat you. You belong with me now," he declares. "That is how your humans say, correct?"

"Close enough," I giggle as he pulls me into his arms.

CHAPTER TWELVE
18 Months Ago

VARIOS

"New girl requires assistance," Clements calls out.

"I shall attend her next," I reply as I clip together the last two cables in the cooling cabinet. Flicking the switch, the lighting for server XL049 returns to green from the previously obnoxious orange flicker.

I slide back out of the racking, raising to full height.

"Do you understand her problem?" I ask as I brush the dust from my hands onto the wipes before dropping them into the trash receptacle.

"No. Humans." He shrugs as if that answers my question.

"I have never interacted with a human," I say.

The truth is, before I took this posting on Callisto I had never heard of a human. Never seen one, nor spoken to one.

"Your RenChip has been updated?" Clements asks.

I nod. "Correct."

"Then, all is well." He turns to leave pausing in the doorway to the server room. "Human females are small. Attempt not to scare her."

"Scare her?"

Clements gestures at my height before he offers me a sympathetic smile and leaves.

<//MERRY&BRIGHT>

I navigate the halls of Police HQ, checking my Glass for the client's location—Forensic Lab 3.

As I step inside the lift a voice calls out, "Hold the door."

Placing my palm on the sensor, the doors stay wide as a small, human female clambers inside, one hand holding an eReader, and the other clutching a noodle box to her chest.

"Thanks," she sighs as she returns her head back to her reading.

"You are most welcome." I incline my head.

The lift chimes, the doors slowly humming closed before we rise to the next floor.

She shifts from foot to foot, standing close enough that I can feel the warmth radiating from her. Her blue scrubs and white lab coat disguise her form, but her smell is undeniable. Her sweetness fills the small elevator until it consumes me. I can taste her in the air.

Something inside me shifts, my heart thrums loudly in my chest as if trying to escape. I fight to keep my hands fisted at my sides.

Fsstik. I swallow to clear my parched throat.

She flicks her long hair over her shoulder, kicking up her scent even stronger. Her hair shines like rays of sunshine reflecting off precious stones.

Her scent wraps around me, taking a hold. I hold my breath, closing my eyes inside my goggles in a desperate attempt to calm myself, not sure what is overcoming me.

I sway forward, my body instinctively leaning towards her. Yearning for her.

<////JJ_HYND>

My hand reaches forwards, my long, slender fingers mere millimetres from tangling in her hair. The lift halts, the doors opening with a hiss of cool air.

"Thanks again," she calls over her shoulder, not looking up from her eReader. "It's Ali, by the way."

"Ah-lee." I sample her name on my tongue. I watch as her hips shift side to side as she walks away, my trousers suddenly feeling rather tight against my cock.

I'm so distracted, I forget to exit the lift before the doors close behind her, and I'm left trying to adjust my cock through my pants before anyone can witness.

Her sweet scent still lingers.

"Mate," I whisper to myself.

<///MERRY&BRIGHT>

ACKNOWLEDGEMENTS

Merry Christmas and thank you for reading.

Staying on theme with this book, I will try to keep the acknowledgements short and sweet.

It was only a matter of time before I made the cross over the dark side, and it has been an absolute delight.

I have long been a connoisseur of monster and alien romance alike, lurking behind the pages as a reader. To finally cross over to the other side and bring my own little flair to the genre has been so much fun and incredibly festive—although it does mean I've been in Christmas mode for most of the year! I apologise to my family and friends for being annoyingly festive.

Thank you to my partner who continues to support and encourage my writing—even despite some of my more unhinged creative ideas—and for listening to me describe alien anatomy in explicit detail.

Thank you to **Ali Evers**, Author of 'Taken by the Wisps', who continues to be one of my closest author friends. I hope you enjoy the not-so-subtle Easter Egg I left for you in this book.

Thank you to Beth at **Wings and Words** for managing the ARC campaign for Merry & Bright! And all the lovely readers in your community of whom I have found some lovely new friends.

Thank you to my incredible editor Becca, **The Proof Fairy**, who has been here giggling away as she proofread Merry & Bright. I truly appreciate all your efforts and putting up with all my last-minute additions.

Special thanks to Chloe who helped prompt a very particular scene—she knows what she did.

Finally, thank you to my parents who have told me they won't read this one as its pornographic.

Happy Reading,

J J Hynd

<///MERRY&BRIGHT>

MEET THE AUTHOR

J. J. Hynd is a Londoner who ran away to the North. A single parent with a short attention span and even less free time, they write stories that are quick to read but still pack a punch. Perfect for fellow burnt-out parents. They write about lovers in space, alien crime lords, murderous AI's, the occasional dinosaur, and barbarian kings.

Tiktok.com/authorjhynd
Instagram.com/authorjjhynd
Linktr.ee/jjhynd

<///JJ_HYND>

ALSO BY J J HYND

ISS ROMANCE SERIES

A Long Way Home

Alex thought she had outrun her old life, that was until her old life came knocking...

Alexandra Peake has a problem. A few, actually.
First there is her ex-husband who turned up out of the blue and is currently pounding his fist against the tiny glass window of the airlock door. Then there is the fact she is trapped on the side of the door currently venting the remains of a breathable atmosphere into the vacuum of space. Plus, she really misses her cat, Tiggie.

Matthias Müller has one problem - How to save his wife.

PRAISE FOR *A LONG WAY HOME*

" It's like someone trapped you in a sleek, slightly malfunctioning spaceship with your ex, threw in unresolved feelings and zero personal space, and said, "Good luck, babe." And honestly? I ate it up." - Ali Evers, author of *Taken by the Wisps*

" If you're looking for something that blends the best of romance and sci-fi, and with more on the horizon, then make sure you check out A Long Way Home! (Did I mention there's some zero-G spice?" - SM Campbell, author of *The Widow's Monster*

Printed in Dunstable, United Kingdom